THE RESCUE QUILT:
A Quilting Cozy

THE RESCUE QUILT: A Quilting Cozy

Carol Dean Jones

Carol Dean Jones, 1938-

Published by Carol Dean Jones, September 2015

ISBN 978-1-329-50940-5

Cover quilt, *The Rescue Quilt*, by Carol Dean Jones

Cover photograph by Woodberry Bowen, Elegant Portraits, Lumberton, North Carolina

Author's Website: http://caroldeanjones.wordpress.com

OTHER BOOKS IN THE QUILTING COZY SERIES
By Carol Dean Jones

TIE DIED (February 2013)

RUNNING STITCHES (May 2013)

SEA BOUND (October 2013)

PATCHWORK CONNECTION (March 2014)

STITCHED TOGETHER (July 2014)

MOON OVER THE MOUNTAIN (January 2015)

Dedicated to Mollye

ACKNOWLEDGEMENTS

My sincere appreciation goes to Janice Packard and Joyce Marlane Frazier for all their encouragement, critiques, and editorial suggestions along the way.

I would also like to thank Sharon Rose who, along with Janice and Joyce, tirelessly combed through this manuscript for those pesky errors that evade the author's eye.

Thank you, dear friends, for all your support, encouragement, and assistance. You've made this project fun.

Chapter 1

Sarah chose a table by the window so she could watch for Sophie. A red SUV pulled up in front of the café displaying a sign identifying it as the "Pup Mobile." Sarah sighed and looked at her watch, wondering what was keeping Sophie. The waitress glanced at the vehicle as she waited for Sarah's order. "I'll just have coffee until my friend gets here," Sarah said as she turned to take another look outside. "Wait," she said with astonishment. "That's my friend getting out of that SUV, but why...?"

Moments later Sophie entered the café and hurried to the table as quickly as her new titanium knee would permit. "Hi Toots," she announced, using the annoying pet term she learned from her ex-fiancé, Cornelius Higginbottom.

"Don't Toots me," Sarah teased, "and what's with the sign painted on your new SUV?"

"Actually that's a magnetized sheet that I just slap on when I'm working."

"Working?" Sarah responded with surprise. She wondered if she'd missed an important chapter in Sophie's life while she was away at her quilting retreat in Tennessee. "Sit down and tell me what's going on."

Sophie unwrapped the hot pink scarf she had twisted around her neck, pulled off her matching cap and gloves, and removed her coat to reveal her new chartreuse running suit. "Do you like it?" she asked as she slowly spun her short, rotund body around giving Sarah a view from all angles.

"It's adorable, Sophie. Now, what do you mean *working*?"

Sophie signaled for the waitress and took a few minutes perusing the menu. "How are your bacon burgers?" she asked.

7

Before the waitress could respond, Sarah said, "I would guess they're the same as the ones you've had every week for the past ten years. Order and tell me what's going on."

"You're getting really pushy in your old age," Sophie grumbled. She ordered the burger and added fried onions and cheddar cheese as she always did.

After sitting and looking at one another for a moment, Sarah raised both eyebrows and said, "So?"

"Okay, you're not going to rest until I tell you the whole story, so here goes. My friend Maria called while you were away and asked me to give her a hand. You know her, right?"

"Yes, I know her from classes at the community center. And doesn't she have that granddaughter who was written up in the local paper last month?"

"That's right. Kelly is her granddaughter and Maria is a volunteer driver for a local animal rescue organization."

"And the Pup Mobile?" Sarah asked.

"I'm getting there. Be patient." Sophie took a sip of her coffee and added two more sugar packets. "Okay, a few weeks ago," she continued, "Kelly asked her grandmother to pick up a little dog from the shelter and drive him out to her farm. Kelly was going to foster him until his forever family got settled in their new home."

"And Maria asked you to go with her?" Sarah interjected, attempting to move the story along.

"Actually, she asked me to drive. Her car was in the shop."

"Ah. And you did?"

"I did. We picked this little fellow up and put his crate in the backseat of my SUV. He was a cute little guy with long hair, a squished up face, and a cute little button nose. His name was Buddy." Sarah smiled, enjoying this rarely seen side of Sophie. "Anyway," Sophie continued, "as we were driving, Maria told me about her volunteer job providing transportation for this group called Sheila's Shuttle."

"Who do they transport exactly?" Sarah asked, still not clear how the story fit together.

"Maria drives dogs mostly, sometimes cats. She takes them to no-kill shelters, to foster homes, and sometimes she takes newly adopted ones to their forever homes. Sometimes she just takes them to meet the next driver along the way to their final destination. She said there's a whole network of volunteers who provide rescue transportation all over the country."

"Hmm," Sarah responded thoughtfully, "Are you thinking of adopting one of these dogs?"

"You know better than that. I can't take care of a dog."

"You certainly could if…"

"Sarah, do you want to hear my story or not?"

"Sorry Sophie. Please finish your story. "

"Okay, here's what I'm doing…"

At that moment, Sophie's cell phone rang and she pulled it out of her pocket and looked at the display. "It's Timmy," she announced excitedly. Timmy was her son who had been working on the Alaska pipeline for the past thirty-five years. "Timmy, I'm so glad you called," Sarah heard her say. "Have you turned in your retirement papers yet?"

Sarah stood up and walked to the counter to get a newspaper and to give her friend some privacy. Sophie, older than Sarah by a few years, wasn't in the best of physical condition, and Sarah wondered what she was planning. She was beginning to realize that it probably had something to do with rescuing animals. She hoped so. Sophie was a warm and caring person who tried to hide behind a rough exterior, but Sarah knew she had a tender heart.

Sarah met Sophie the day she moved into Cunningham Village, and they had become close friends, with Sophie helping her make the difficult transition into a retirement community. At that time, they lived across the street from each other, but Sarah had since moved into a house in a newer section of the village, which catered to couples. And after twenty years as a widow, Sarah was now officially part of a couple. On a snowy New Year's Eve, she had married Charles, a retired policeman whom she adored and who adored her.

"I'm so excited, Timmy," Sarah heard her friend squeal from her table as she was saying goodbye to her son. Sophie signaled for Sarah to return to the table and announced with excitement, "He turned in his retirement papers, and he'll be home in a couple of months. I can hardly believe it," she added looking relieved. "I was beginning to think he'd never leave Alaska."

"Did he say anything about his plans once he gets here?" Sarah asked, wondering if he planned to make his home in Middletown.

"Only that he can't wait to see Martha," she responded with a mischievous grin. Martha was Sarah's forty-five year old daughter. She and Tim had met the previous year when he was visiting his mother and they had instantly hit it off. Sophie and Sarah kidded about becoming mutual mothers-in-law, but neither Tim nor Martha would discuss the possibility.

"So," Sarah began. "Do you think you can finally tell me what you and your decorated SUV are up to?"

* * *

"So she's going to be driving rescued dogs?" Charles repeated with a chuckle. "Your outrageous friend is full of surprises." He shook his head in mock skepticism, but his eyes were twinkling with amusement.

"Well, here's what she told me," Sarah began. "Her friend Maria who has been volunteering as a driver for a local rescue organization asked Sophie to drive her on a couple of her assignments while her car was in the shop."

"Do we know this Maria?"

"Yes. Maria Wilcox. You met her at the pool last month. She was swimming laps next to you during my water aerobics class. She has a very special granddaughter. This young woman, I believe her name is Kelly, has a farm outside of town. A few years ago she took in a goat that had come to the attention of Animal Control. He'd been neglected and abused for years and was practically dead. She nursed him back to health and gave him a loving home."

"I read an article about her a few months ago," Charles responded. "She's turned her farm into a foster home for abandoned or abused animals of all kinds. She's got a few horses, a miniature pony, two goats, and lots of dogs and cats. The reporter was asking for donations for food and medical care. I was thinking about sending them a check."

"Yes," Sarah responded, "I read that article and I think we should. Anyway, back to Sophie's story. She drove Maria for a week or so until Maria's car was repaired and she really enjoyed it. So, when Maria told her she wanted to take a couple of months off and visit her sister Caterina in Italy, Sophie volunteered to take the runs for her while she was away. She's been doing it for a couple of weeks now and she loves it. She even has a fancy sign on the side of her SUV identifying herself as the 'Pup Mobile.'"

"No cats?"

"No, she's allergic."

"Won't this involve lots of driving? That article said the animals come from all over the country."

"She'll be part of a network. I don't think they have to drive more than a couple of hours. The volunteers tag-team when the locations are far apart."

"I've got to admire Sophie for taking this on at her age," Charles responded thoughtfully.

"Timothy called today and he's turned in his retirement papers and will be back here in a few months. I'm sure he'll help his mom if she needs him."

Charles laughed. "If she can get him away from your daughter. Martha told me that she and Tim have been on the phone almost every night since she visited him in Alaska. I think we'll be hearing wedding bells before long."

"We'll see," Sarah responded with a trace of hesitation in her voice. Charles looked at her inquisitively, but didn't ask if she had reservations.

"Anyway," Sarah continued, ignoring his questioning look, "Sophie wants me to ride along with her tomorrow. She's taking two young dogs to the Greyhound rescue in Hamilton. We'll be gone for several hours. I want to stop at the mall and, if I know Sophie, she'll want to work in lunch somewhere along the way."

"That works for me," Charles responded. "I'm going to be working tomorrow. I'd like to talk to a few of the neighbors around that crime scene over on the east side. Sometimes fresh eyes can spot an inconsistency. It doesn't seem logical that no one saw or heard anything considering ..." Charles stopped in the middle of the sentence. He rarely discussed the details of the cases he worked on, and this one involved senior citizens and was particularly grizzly. There's lots of depravity out there, and my lovely wife doesn't need those pictures in her head, he told himself.

Charles, retired from Middletown Police Department, had been helping his old lieutenant from time to time. Primarily, he just knocked on doors and looked for possible leads which he'd then pass on. He missed police work and enjoyed the feeling of being included, even at this minimal level.

"There's something else I wanted to ask you," Charles began somewhat awkwardly.

"What is it?" Sarah responded, sitting down at the kitchen table with him.

"Well, I was trying to surprise you with an anniversary party at the community center."

"Oh Charles, what a sweet thing to do..."

"...but I'm having trouble pulling all the pieces together," he continued. "I'm not much good at this kind of thing, so..."

"So, you'd like me to help with the planning?"

"Actually, I'd like for you to take over. I've made a real mess of it," he admitted hanging his head in exaggerated embarrassment. "Please?"

Sarah laughed. "Well, if it's not too late to change what plans you've already made, I'd really like to have it right here at home."

"Great!" Charles responded, looking relieved. "You've solved one of the problems already. The center was already booked for New Year's Eve and I had a caterer all set up with no place to cater."

Sarah laughed as she stood to wrap her arms around her very thoughtful husband. "Well now she does. Bring me your invitation list and I'll take a look at it."

"Invitation list?"

"No list?"

"No, but I've mentioned it to a few people," he responded looking embarrassed.

"Okay, let's sit down and make a list of everything that needs to be done, and you'll tell me which of those things are already arranged. Let's start with who you might have invited." Charles came up with about ten people he remembered mentioning it to and together they listed another ten they would like to invite. "Twenty people will fit in the house comfortably if we borrow a few folding chairs from Ruth at the quilt shop."

"She has extra chairs?"

"Yes, for her classes, but now that I think about it, we should invite her too and perhaps ..." *What have I gotten myself into?* Sarah asked herself as she set the list aside and poured a cup of coffee. *And I haven't even started my Christmas shopping...*

Chapter 2

The next morning, Sophie woke up early and called Sarah. "Let's leave now and we can stop for breakfast after we drop the dogs off," she suggested.

"Sorry, Sophie. I just got up and can't be ready for at least a half hour," she yawning as she started the coffee.

"How about I go pick up the dogs and swing back here to pick you up. Will that give you enough time?"

"Sounds good," Sarah responded, knowing that Sophie would spend extra time at the kennel talking with the staff. As she was hanging up, Charles came into the kitchen and kissed her on the cheek.

"What sounds good?" Charles asked.

Sarah caught him up on Sophie's plans for the morning. "You're on your own for breakfast," she added as she poured him a cup of coffee. "I'll take my coffee with me," she added, pulling a travel mug out of the cabinet.

Sarah took a quick shower and had just finished dressing when she heard Sophie pull into the driveway. "Tell Sophie I'm on my way," she called to Charles.

As Sarah approached the Pup Mobile a few minutes later, Sophie was just stepping out and heading toward the back of the vehicle. "Come back here and look at these adorable puppies," Sophie said as she lifted the hatch. "Meet Tilly and Tom. Aren't they just too cute?"

Tilly was a pretty little white Greyhound puppy with patches of black scattered here and there. Her large ears stood straight up when Sarah spoke to her, but Tom moved to the back of the crate and peeked at her over his sister's back. "Jackie said they're very timid, especially with strangers."

14

"Is that a cast on his leg?" Sarah asked with a frown.

"Yes, the vet discovered a fracture when he was examining him," Sophie responded as the two women got into the car and snapped their seatbelts. "No one knows how he got it. They belonged to this couple who was killed in an automobile accident on the Interstate a few weeks ago. A real tragedy. Her son took the puppies into the Humane Society."

"I guess no one in the family could take them..."

"He flew in from New York. That's all I know, but they'll be fine. They're on their way to Hamilton Greyhound Rescue. Jackie said they'll be easy to place. They have a waiting list for puppies. It's the older dogs that sometimes take longer."

The trip was uneventful, which gave Sophie and Sarah time to visit.

When they arrived at their destination, Sarah was surprised to find they were at a private home in the suburbs. "I thought we were going to take them to a shelter."

"No, this is a family that volunteers to foster greyhounds until their forever homes are found." A woman in jeans and a tee-shirt came hurrying out to the car as she pulled on a down jacket. Her red curls sparkled in the sunshine and a broad smile stretched across her face.

"Let me see those baby dolls," she cried as she approached the rear of the car. Once the hatch was opened, she ooh'd and aah'd as she opened the crate and removed little Tilly. "Jackie told me they're very timid, but look at this one! She's already licking my face."

"You might find her brother to be the timid one. He has an injured leg and he seems very shy," Sarah offered, but when the woman rested her hand inside the crate, Tom timidly approached and allowed her to pet him.

"I'm Fran, by the way," the woman said by way of introduction. Sarah and Sophie introduced themselves and helped her return Tilly to the crate.

"Can you manage that alone?" Sarah asked as Fran lifted the crate of pups.

"Oh I'm a tough one," she responded. "I've got five more of these characters inside, but these are the only puppies. I'll have to be careful not to get too attached. They'll be gone within a week. We have a waiting list for the little ones." Sarah walked Fran to her door and held it open for her. She spotted two larger dogs gated in what appeared to be the dining room. They were tall and thin with pointed ears and curious eyes.

"You must love your work," she commented as she was closing the screen door behind Fran.

"You bet I do. They come in here sad and frightened, but it doesn't take long to get them smiling. It just takes love." From the twinkle in Fran's eyes, Sarah knew this woman had lots of love to give.

On the drive home, Sarah asked Sophie about funding for the foster homes. "Who pays for all this?" she asked.

"It's primarily volunteer. These rescue organizations have shelters but they get overcrowded and foster homes can take the dogs when the organization doesn't have room or when the dogs need to be in a home environment."

"Don't all dogs need that?"

"Sure, but it's not always possible. Jackie at the Humane Society told me that sometimes it's critical, like newborn pups who need more care than the staff can manage. Sometimes," Sophie continued, "the animals need special care after some kind of medical procedure. Or sometimes the animal might have behavior problems that a specially trained foster person could help with in order to get the animal ready for adoption. But most of the time, it's simply due to overcrowding. They go to the foster homes while the agency looks for permanent homes." Sophie went on to talk about the no-kill shelters and quoted some facts about needs and the lack of resources.

"How did you learn all this?" Sarah asked surprised at all the details Sophie had in her head.

"One of the first runs I took for Maria was a little two-year old Shih Tzu, an adorable little fluff ball, and I just fell in love. They had told me she'd been in the shelter for a few weeks and was very timid and frightened, but she was just a peach with me. She seemed to love having attention. I moved her little crate up in the front seat and belted it in so I could talk to her. Anyway, that's when I decided that I might like to help out by doing some short term fostering, and I signed up for their orientation. I'm on the list now but they haven't needed me yet."

They were quiet for the next few miles. Sarah was thinking about Sophie and the little Shih Tzu and how difficult it must be for a foster caregiver to part with these little dogs once a forever home was found for them. She asked Sophie about this.

"One lady told me that it's hard to say goodbye, but she reminds herself that when a home is found for one, she is freed up to save another one."

Sarah looked over at Sophie and saw a tenderness she hadn't noticed before. My friend has found her niche, she told herself with a smile.

* * *

"How did your detecting go?" Sarah asked as she and Charles sat down to dinner later that evening.

"It was most unsuccessful. I detected nothing. And how did your rescuing go?"

"Most successfully," she responded enthusiastically. She went on to tell Charles about the puppies and about Fran. "It takes a very special person to take on all that responsibility," she reflected thinking about Fran's life.

About that time Barney slowly made his way across the kitchen floor and sat by Sarah's chair. "Is he limping?" Sarah asked, noting that he was having trouble walking.

"I've noticed that mostly when he first gets up. It reminds me of the way I feel after I've been sitting awhile. Our aging joints are rebelling."

"I suppose he could have some joint pain. I don't know how old he is, but from what the vet said when I got him, he could be approaching eleven or twelve at this point."

"Let's take him in for a check-up," Charles responded. "It's about time for his shots and I'm sure they have something that will help him."

As they were clearing away the dinner dishes, Charles asked about the party.

"I picked up the invitations while we were out today, and I hope to get them in the mail tomorrow. Sophie has already talked to several of our friends, and it looks like most of them will be coming, although some of the older people said they might not stay until midnight. It'll be a good crowd."

"Have you thought about what we'll feed all these folks?" Charles asked.

"Sophie and I talked about that today. I think we should offer wine and cheese along with an array of finger foods. We can't accommodate that many people for dinner without putting tables all over the house, and I think it'll be more fun to have the food spread around so that people can circulate. What do you think?"

"I agree. Give Kendra's Katering a call. She did a fantastic time with our gourmet picnic last year."

"Yes, that's on my list," Sarah responded. "I'll have her work up a menu."

"And we're doing this on our actual anniversary, right?"

"Yes, New Year's Eve."

"Champagne at midnight?"

"Absolutely," she responded with a smile.

"And a kiss?"

"I wouldn't miss it."

Charles pulled his wife into a gentle hug; Barney limped over and nosed his way between them.

Chapter 3

Sophie was in her third week of taking Maria's runs and had met more dogs than she had known in her lifetime. *How could I have gone all these years without a dog*, she wondered, looking at the mournful face of the little Cocker Spaniel who had been abandoned when his owner moved out of state. He was picked up sitting on the porch of the empty house where he had been waiting for them to return. A neighbor had finally noticed him and called Animal Control.

"Where are we taking him?" Sarah asked Sophie, glad she had been asked to ride along again.

"He's been adopted by a family in Madison, Wisconsin. We're meeting the next driver about an hour from here. The poor little fellow has been on the road for two days already."

"You said he started out in Dallas? How did this Wisconsin family find out about him?"

"They have a young boy who's been surfing the internet looking at rescue sites. He fell in love with this little fellow, and they were able to make arrangements for him to be transported north."

Sarah was quiet for a while thinking about how excited the boy must be. She wondered about his home and finally asked Sophie, "How do the folks in Dallas know they're sending him to a good home?"

"A rescue organization in Madison will have done a home study and reported back to Dallas. They're very careful about who adopts these dogs. They've been through enough already." Sarah looked into the vanity mirror and saw the little face looking toward the front seat. She figured he was wondering what was in store for him. She thought about all the nights he spent on the porch of the abandoned house waiting for the people he loved to return. Tears began to burn her eyes, and she blinked hard to clear them away.

Once she got home, Sarah found herself unable to get the little dog out of her mind. She hoped he would soon forget what he'd been through and would become a happy member of his new family. Barney, sensing her mood, laid his head on her lap and rolled his eyes up mournfully. As usual, her sad thoughts vanished. She squeezed his face between her hands and said, "You're one lucky dog, do you know that?"

* * *

"Mrs. Ward, this is Sheila from the shuttle service. There's a dog at the Humane Society that we think would do better out at Kelly's farm. Are you available to take her out there this afternoon?"

"Sure, I'll be right there," Sophie responded.

"You know what to do -- just pick her up and drive on out to Kelly's farm. She'll be expecting you."

Within a few minutes, Sophie was ready to go. Although there was a chill in the air, it was a beautiful afternoon and Sophie was glad to be getting out. It was a short trip to the shelter and on out to Kelly's farm on the outskirts of Middletown, and she knew she could easily be home before dark. She turned the radio on and found herself humming to the easy listening station.

At the shelter, she was surprised to see how restless the dog was. She was pacing in the cage as if eager to get out. The staff had difficulty transferring her to a crate, but she seemed to settle down somewhat once they lifted her into the back of Sophie's SUV.

"She's beautiful," Sophie commented despite the dirty and matted fur. She appeared to be primarily white with a long plumed tail that curved above her back. Sophie reached in to pet her and the dog gave her a pleading look. "What is it, girl?"

Sophie asked, wishing the dog could speak. They latched the crate and lowered the hatch.

"She's been agitated since we picked her up," Jackie explained.

"Where did you find her?"

"We had calls from several shops in town reporting that she was clawing at their doors, but no one could figure out what she wanted. Once we got her to the shelter we tried to feed her, but she refused. She just paced constantly and tried to scratch her way out."

After Jackie went back inside, Sophie lifted the hatch and spoke softly to the dog. "It's going to be okay, girl. I'm taking you to a safe place." She hoped that Kelly's vet could figure out why she was so agitated.

She wondered what kind of dog she was. Jackie had said she was a mixed breed and perhaps she had some Malamute in her background with that full tail curling up over her back. "But she's much smaller than a Malamute," Jackie had added. "Maybe she has some Husky or even some Border Collie. She only weighs thirty-five pounds. We'll see what Kelly's vet thinks."

Her fur was matted, but looked soft. Sophie could see light brown markings on the top of her head and across her back. "I'll bet you'll be beautiful once you've had a bath," Sophie said again speaking gently. "Do you have a name?" The dog had a well-worn leather collar but no identification. The staff's vet had estimated her age at seven or eight.

Once they were on the road, Sophie thought the dog had calmed down; at least she wasn't whimpering. As Sophie approached the edge of town, she realized the gas tank was low, so she pulled into the next station, not sure how long it would be before she passed another one. She raised the rear hatch to let the cool breeze into the back of the SUV and proceeded to fill the gas tank. She had left the radio on thinking it might have a soothing effect on the dog.

Once the tank was filled and the credit card transaction completed, she walked around to the back to close the hatch and was horrified to see that the door to the crate was open and the latch was snapped completely off. The dog was crouched ready to spring. Sophie was frozen in place.

A moment later a white muddy streak shot out of the car and began running up the side of the road away from town. Sophie yelled, "Come back, come back," but to no avail. She hurried into the car, started it up, and followed the dog. She was able to catch up with her quickly.

She knew she wouldn't be able to coax her back into the car, so she decided to just follow at a safe distance, hoping she didn't turn and run through the field. She reached for her cell phone to call for help, but it slipped to the floor and she didn't dare reach for it. "Who would I call anyway?" she asked herself aloud.

A few miles up the road, the dog appeared to be tiring. Sophie hoped this meant she would be willing to get into the car soon. Suddenly she noticed the dog had stopped completely and was looking back at the car. Sophie slowed down as she approached, praying she would simply get into the car. She had already decided not to try to put her in the crate, but instead just let her get in the backseat. She would coax her in with one of the dog biscuits she kept on hand for just such situations.

But to her surprise, as soon as she was close, the dog turned and started running up a side road that intersected with the highway. Sophie quickly turned on the road and followed. The two resumed their previous pattern, but this time much slower. The unpaved road followed a stream and the terrain was becoming hilly and wooded. They both slowed down, and the dog stopped momentarily to drink from the stream. Sophie stopped, but the dog immediately resumed her trek with renewed determination.

Sophie was concerned when the dog made another turn. She found herself on a deeply rutted dirt road. She now had to go very slowly and was afraid she would lose the dog, but was surprised to see her slow down. She appeared to be pacing herself to the car. Is she leading me somewhere? Sophie wondered.

Five or ten minutes later the dog took another turn into the overgrown yard of a rustic log cabin. She ran up to the door, her tail now wagging as she barked enthusiastically and scratched at the door. Sophie got out of the car but was very stiff from sitting so long. She reached for her cane, which she kept in the car for times like this when walking was more difficult.

Sophie crossed the rutted yard cautiously and noticed that the dog was looking back at her as if to make sure she was following behind. She carefully climbed the steps and crossed the rustic porch to the door. She didn't think anyone was home, or they would have responded to all the noise the dog had made. She knocked hard but heard no sounds inside.

She walked over to the window and pressed her face against the glass. Her screams echoed across the countryside.

* * *

"We're on our way, Sophie. I'll stay on the cell phone with you until we get there. What did the police say when you called them?"

"They wanted the address, but I have no idea where I am. The officer said they were able to identify my cell phone location and they're on their way. They asked questions about the man, but I couldn't tell them anything. I told them I didn't go in, but I could see a man lying on the floor in a pool of blood." Sarah heard the panic in Sophie's voice, and she knew her friend was fighting to hang on. "What should I do," Sophie asked in a quivering voice.

"We'll be there soon, honey. Just stay in your car."

"How will you find me?" Sophie asked, her voice still shaking.

"Charles called dispatch and got the GPS location," Sarah responded. "It says we'll be there in eighteen minutes. What about the dog? Is she in the car with you?"

"No, she's on the porch curled up on a dirty old blanket and looks right at home. I'm sure she lives here. Do you suppose she went all the way into town trying to get help?" Sophie sounded more in control when she was talking about the dog.

"It sounds like it, Sophie. Tell me about the dog. What does she look like?" Sarah was hoping to take her friend's mind off the body at least momentarily.

"She's not very big. I think Jackie said she's about thirty-five pounds. I think she's mostly white but she's so dirty it's hard to tell for sure." Her voice cracked again as she added, "At the shelter they said she wouldn't eat or drink. I wish..." Sophie stopped mid-sentence. "Oh Sarah, I hear sirens. Stay on the phone until they get here."

"I will, are they..."

"They just turned in," Sophie exclaimed excitedly. "Two police cars and an ambulance. An ambulance? Do you think the man might still be alive? I never thought of that. Maybe I should have..." Sophie's voice was escalating.

"Sophie, there's nothing you could have done. The medics are there now. Go ahead and open your car door."

"Are you Sophie Ward?" Sarah heard someone ask.

"Yes," she responded with a shaking voice, still holding the phone in her hand.

"Sophie, we'll be there soon," Sarah assured her as Sophie disconnected the phone.

"Charles, that's our turn up there on the right."

"I know," he responded in a tone Sarah wasn't accustomed to hearing. She turned to look at him and realized his face was tense with worry. "I'm just relieved that the police are there. I was afraid whoever did this was still around."

"You didn't say a word," Sarah responded with surprise. "Why didn't you tell me?"

"I didn't want to scare either one of you."

"I wouldn't have said anything to Sophie."

"She would have heard it in your voice, Sarah. We did tell her to lock herself in the car. That's about all we could do."

Charles took a sharp right and headed up the narrow dirt road traveling much faster than Sophie had earlier that day. Within minutes, they arrived at the house and parked among the other vehicles.

"Can I help you," an officer called out as he walked toward their car.

"We're friends of Mrs. Ward. Is she inside?" He pulled out his department identification, regretting that it wasn't the shiny badge he had flashed for so many years.

"Fine, go on in."

At the door, he leaned in and asked if it was okay to enter the crime scene. "It's not a crime scene," the officer in charge responded, motioning for them to come in. "It was just this old guy's time," the officer responded.

"What about the blood?" Sarah asked.

"Probably banged his head on something when he fell."

On what? Sarah thought but decided not to say. She looked around and didn't see anything he might have fallen against. She looked at Charles and saw a deep frown as he looked at the body.

"Do you know who he is?" Charles asked.

"Yeah," the officer responded. "That's old Earl Hawkins. He's been living alone back here for years."

About that time, the dog crept into the room and laid next to the man's feet. She let out a deep mournful howl.

"Get that filthy mutt out of here," the officer yelled to one of the officers impatiently.

26

"I'll get her," Sophie called out defensively from the corner of the room. "She's my responsibility." She hurried over and gently led the dog by her collar. The dog willingly followed Sophie as if she were beginning to understand the futility of remaining with her master. Sarah met them at the door and the two women, followed by the forlorn dog, headed for Sophie's car.

"What are you going to do with her?" Sarah asked.

"Take her on to Kelly's farm, I guess. What else can I do?"

"I don't think you should be driving alone. We'll go with you."

When Charles finally joined them, he explained that the investigator needed to take Sophie's statement, but was willing to wait until the next day. "We'll go with you," Charles said. "Now, how shall we juggle these cars?"

"Let's take both cars down to the main highway," Sarah suggested. "We can park Sophie's car in that mini-mall we passed, and the three of us can drive on up to Kelly's farm."

"Wait," Sophie interjected. "We've all been through too much, and it'll be dark before long. Let's just go home. I'll keep the dog overnight and let the shelter know what happened."

"Are you sure you want to do that, Sophie? She'll have to be walked, and fed…"

"I can handle it. Will you loan me a leash and some of Barney's food?"

"Of course, but I have a better idea. How about I come spend the night with you?" Sarah asked.

"A sleep-over?" Sophie responded, looking relieved. "That sounds like fun."

Charles winked at Sarah, knowing that she was concerned about leaving Sophie alone after the trauma of finding the body, not to mention leaving her with the responsibility of caring for a strange dog.

Sarah got behind the wheel of Sophie's car and her friend handed her the keys without question. Sophie then got into the back seat with the dog who was now stretched out and resigned to whatever fate was in store for her. She had lost her master and nothing else mattered.

Charles pulled out ahead of them and lead the way to the main road and back to Cunningham Village.

Chapter 4

"Let's head out to Kelly's farm first and then on to the police station," Charles suggested when he called Sarah the next morning. He had waited until after nine, hoping she and Sophie had been able to get some sleep. "How's the dog doing?"

"She's just lying on the kitchen floor. She appears to be resting, but I think she's just resigned to the fact that her person is gone. She looks depressed."

"Did she eat any of the food you brought?"

"She took a few bites out of Sophie's hand last night. I'm hoping she'll perk up when she gets to the farm."

"I'll pick you up in about a half hour if that works for you gals."

"Perfect. We're dressed and having coffee. We'll see you then."

Sarah slipped her cell phone back into her pocket and picked up a slice of Sophie's pumpkin-nut bread. She put a thin smear of butter on it. Sophie pushed the jam in her direction and asked, "What did he say?"

"He'll be here around ten. I'm going to take the dog for a short walk before we leave. Do you have any idea what her name is?"

"None. There's no identification on her collar, and the shelter staff said she didn't have a microchip."

"That's too bad. I had Barney chipped right away when I adopted him and got him registered with the microchip folks. That way if he's ever found wandering like this poor dog was, any vet or shelter can find out who he belongs to."

"It's pretty unlikely that your Barney will ever wander. He knows a good thing when he sees it," Sophie chuckled. "That's one spoiled dog. Back to your question, I think her name is Drusilla."

"Drusilla?" Sarah's eyebrows flew high on her forehead as she responded.

"Yes. I tried out a bunch of names on her last night, and she didn't react until I said 'Drusilla,' and then she gave me this look." Sophie tilted her head to the side and looked at Sarah wide-eyed.

"Perhaps she thought you'd lost your mind. That's a strange name for a dog."

"Well, it was good enough for my Aunt Drusilla," Sophie announced indignantly with her fists on her sizable hips.

"Oops, sorry." Sarah stood up and reached for her jacket. "Come on Drusilla, let's take a walk." The dog didn't respond.

"Now that I hear you saying it," Sophie reluctantly admitted, "I guess it's not the best name for her. What do you think of *Emma*?"

"Oh, I like that!" Sarah responded looking pleased. Turning to the dog she said, "Come on, Emma. Let's go." To their surprise the dog stood up, stretched, and followed Sarah to the door. "I think that's it," Sarah said giving Sophie a nod.

"I agree, "Sophie responded, "and let's stop at the pet store on our way to Kelly's farm. They have a machine there that you can use to make a name tag. That way her new owner will know what to call her. I think it's important to her."

Sarah sighed and nodded her agreement.

As Sarah and Emma were leaving the house, Charles pulled into the driveway. "Glad you're here," she called to him. Once she got closer, she confided, "I think Sophie needs to talk to you about yesterday. Discovering that body has really upset her, but she doesn't seem to want to talk to me about it. I think she'll talk to you."

"Will do. But first I need my good morning kiss." Sarah glanced around, always a little embarrassed when Charles showed affection in public. Her late husband, Jonathan, had been a very private man and wouldn't as much as hold hands in public, even when they were young. Sarah was slowly getting used to Charles' demonstrative ways and was even learning to enjoy it.

"Are you gals about ready to leave?" he asked.

"Sophie is calling Kelly now to tell her what time we'll be there. I'm going to walk Emma around the block before we leave, and that'll give you and Sophie time to talk."

"Emma?"

"Don't laugh. She was almost named Drusilla."

"Then I'm glad you two settled on Emma. In fact," Charles added, tilting his head and looking at the dog more critically, "she sort of looks like an Emma."

While Sarah walked Emma around the block, Charles and Sophie talked about the night before. Sophie wanted to know what was going to be happening at the police station and Charles described the procedure. "They like to talk to the witnesses right away. They just need to document your description of what happened last night."

"What happened?" Sophie repeated looking confused. "I don't know what happened."

"I just mean things like when you got there, what you saw or didn't see -- things like that. They usually talk to the witnesses at the scene, but they agreed to let us go home and come back this morning."

"I keep thinking about that poor man lying there in that puddle of blood. What do you think happened to him?"

"I don't know, but the police will find out. I'm sure they've started their investigation already. In fact, they might have something to tell us when we get to the station."

"Did you hear the officer say it was probably just the old man's time? Do you think he died of natural causes?" Sophie

31

asked. Charles wasn't accustomed to seeing Sophie looking so intense. She had almost a pleading look on her face.

"I don't know Sophie, but they'll find out. Middletown has some very competent investigators."

"Are you folks about ready to leave?" Sarah hollered from the front door.

Before Charles could respond, Sophie called out, "We're right behind you. Go ahead and get Emma settled in her crate." Turning to Charles, she said, "Thanks for talking to me about it. I feel better. I guess I was picking up some of Emma's concerns."

"Emma probably knows what happened," Charles said speculatively. "Too bad she can't tell us. Anyway, Sarah's waiting. Let's hit the road."

They stopped at the pet store, and Sarah offered to remain in the car with Emma while Sophie and Charles had the identification tag made. When the two returned to the car, they were carrying several bags, two of which were very large. Sophie opened one of the smaller bags and removed a small heart-shaped tag with the name *Emma* engraved on it and a pink leather collar. She snapped the tag onto the collar and replaced Emma's ragged collar with the fresh new one. "There," she said with a smile. "I told you it would fit."

"You were right," Charles said, slipping two fingers under the collar to make sure it wasn't too tight.

"What's in the big bag?" Sarah asked.

"Food," Sophie answered. "Lots of food."

"And a few toys," Charles added grinning.

As they approached the farm, the sun began to shine. There was a light dusting of snow on the fields that sparkled in the sunlight. "It's beautiful out here," Sarah commented. "I love the countryside."

Kelly met them in the driveway when they pulled in and eagerly welcomed Emma to her home. Emma looked around spotting the cows near the fence and started to whine. Kelly gently caressed her head and assured her there was no danger. She snapped her own leash onto Emma's collar and handed Barney's leash back to Sophie. "I'll take her in the house and introduce her around. She'll be fine once she gets the lay of the land. By the way, do you know what her name is?"

"It's Emma," Sophie announced with authority. "It's on that little tag on her collar."

"Oh, good. We often don't know what name these little rescue dogs are accustomed to. Come on, Emma." The dog looked back at Sophie for a moment, then turned and followed Kelly into the house.

Sarah thought she saw Sophie begin to tear up, but decided she must have been mistaken when Sophie turned abruptly and said, "Let's go see the cops."

* * *

"How many times am I going to have to repeat that story?" Sophie demanded, sitting suddenly very straight in her chair and looking indignant.

Officer Reilly, sitting behind his cluttered desk, continued to look directly at Sophie. He repeated his question. "Why were you at the Hawkins house yesterday?"

Sophie signed. "Okay, one more time. I was transporting a dog from the downtown shelter to an animal foster home out past the truck stop. The dog jumped out of the car and I followed her. She ran right up to the house and scratched on the door."

"How long have you known Mr. Hawkins?"

"What?" Sophie shrieked. "You've got to be kidding."

"It's no laughing matter, Mrs. Ward. A man has been murdered."

"Murdered?" Charles spoke up, abruptly interrupting what was beginning to sound like an interrogation.

Officer Reilly turned to Charles with a deep frown. "I'll handle this," he chastised.

"Murdered?" Sophie said, repeating Charles' question. "Yesterday you said he died of natural causes. In fact, I think your exact words were, 'it was just the old man's time.'"

Reilly gave her a cold stare before responding. "We're waiting for the medical examiner's report but, in the meantime, we're looking at other possibilities. So, Mrs. Ward, I'd appreciate your answer to my questions."

"Do I need a lawyer?" she asked in an accusatory tone.

"I don't know, Mrs. Ward. Do you?" Reilly responded raising his left eyebrow high on his forehead.

"My friend here," waving her hand toward Charles, "knows I didn't do it, and he's a famous detective..."

"Wait a minute, Sophie," Charles said, interrupting what was quickly becoming one of Sophie's tirades and not knowing where she was going with it. The three were sitting on folding chairs across from the investigating officer. Charles gently laid his hand on her arm and said, "We're just here so you can answer some questions for them."

"Well, if the man was murdered, then someone needs to be pursuing the real killer and not wasting time asking me stupid questions," she responded, pulling her arm away from him.

"Let's talk about this when we get home, okay?"

Sophie looked at Charles. She knew he had suspicions the previous night when they were all in the man's cabin. Maybe he wants to investigate this on his own, she thought. "Okay," she said softly, deciding to trust what she knew about her friend's husband. "I'll let it go for now, but..."

"Thank you, Sophie," Charles said interrupting her. "Please go on, Officer Reilly. You were asking about Mrs. Ward's involvement."

"Yes," the officer responded, seeming grateful that Charles had put the issue to rest, at least for now. "Why don't you tell your side of the story first, Mr. Parker."

"That's Detective Parker," Sophie interjected proudly.

"Retired," Charles clarified. "Mrs. Ward was transporting the dog from the Humane Society to…"

"I drive the Pup Mobile…" Sophie added.

The officer looked at her for a moment and turned back to Charles. "Go on please."

Charles gave Sophie a look that she read to mean she should remain quiet. "As I was saying," he continued, "she was driving this dog to a foster home outside of town when the dog escaped from the car." He went on to tell how Sophie had followed her to the cabin and saw the body through the window.

"When did you call the police, Mrs. Ward?" he asked.

"I called right away and then I called my friends. They…"

Charles cut in and finished the story about how they told her to get back in her car and lock it until the police arrived. "My wife and I got there just after the police arrived."

"Did anyone touch anything before we got there?"

Sophie, stiffening again and looking irritated said, "Didn't he just tell you I sat in my car until you got there? Of course no one touched anything. None of us were in the house until you arrived."

The officer wrote a few words in the record and then asked, "Was the door locked when you got there, Mrs. Ward?"

Sophie sighed. "I didn't try it. Was it locked when you got there?" she asked in a slightly sarcastic tone.

Officer Reilly ignored the question and made a few more notes in the record.

"Why do you think the dog led you to the cabin?"

Sarah had been quiet up to that point, but she responded to his question, knowing that it could easily set Sophie off again. "We think the dog lived there and was in town trying to get help for her owner."

"Hmm. Seems a bit farfetched," he muttered.

"She seemed right at home once help arrived." Sarah added in a non-confrontational tone.

"Where's the dog now?"

"We took her on to the foster home," Sophie said, not adding that she took her home with her the night before. *None of his business*, she thought defiantly.

Officer Reilly asked a few more questions to clarify the details and finally closed the folder. "Thank you folks for coming in," he said while standing up, which clearly gave the message that the interview was over. As the others reaching for their coats, he added, "Mrs. Ward, don't leave town. We'll be in touch."

Sophie who was in the process of pulling on her gloves, froze. "Don't leave town?" she repeated. "Don't leave town? What is this, a mafia movie? Don't leave town?" Turning to Sarah she added, "It looks like I *do* need a lawyer after all. Get your son-in-law on the phone."

Charles rolled his eyes and gave the officer an apologetic look.

Chapter 5

"How much longer will Maria be gone?" Sarah asked.

"Two or three more months," Sophie responded. Maria had called Sophie to say that she'd decided to extend her vacation. Her sister wanted her to see more of Europe while she was there.

"They've scheduled a cruise that starts in the Mediterranean and goes..." Sophie stopped and picked up a note pad where she had jotted down some of the places Maria told her about. "...from Italy, the ship sails west past Gibraltar and on up the coast, disembarking along the way for shore-excursions in Spain, Portugal, France, and..." looking up, Sophie added, "and I think she said England too, but she was talking so fast I didn't get it all down. Anyway, she said they'll end up in Amsterdam and from there they're taking a train down through Germany and the Bavarian Alps."

"Whew. What a trip," Sarah responded. "That must take weeks, but what a wonderful experience. As long as she's there, she might as well make the most of it."

"I think she wanted to spend more time with her sister too. They hadn't seen each other for the past six or seven years. Her brother-in-law hopes to retire soon and they'll probably move back to the States. In the meantime, this is great for Maria."

"So you'll keep driving the dogs?"

"You bet. She wanted me to call Sheila's Shuttle service and let her know that I'll be continuing to take Maria's runs until she comes home. Actually, I'd forgotten about that. I just got so busy getting things ready for Tim. You know, I'm redoing the guest room so it's not so girly."

"When do you expect him?" Sarah asked, thinking Sophie must still have another month or so.

"He'll be here in late January, but I want to hire someone to paint that room. I don't think my son's going to go for pale lilac," she added chuckling.

"Let me check with Charles. He'll probably do it for you."

The two friends went on to talk about Tim, but they avoided the topic of any potential marriage between their children. Both Timothy and Martha had made it clear they didn't want to discuss the possibility with either of their parents. Martha had traveled to Alaska the previous summer and had returned with few details, despite her mother's gentle prodding.

"What's the big secret anyway," Sophie scoffed.

Sarah didn't respond, but she thought she understood her daughter's reluctance to make a commitment. Martha had a very painful experience in her first marriage – something she was careful to never repeat. *Perhaps she's being a little too careful*, Sarah thought but didn't say.

"We'll have to just pull back, Sophie. They'll talk to us when they're ready."

"So," Sophie said changing the subject, "let's drive over to the hardware store and look at paint chips. I'm not sure what color this room should be."

"Good idea. I need to stop in the fabric store while we're on that side of town."

"More fabric?" Sophie asked. "What's with you quilters anyway? Every time you go into a fabric shop, you come out with bags and bags of fabric. What do you do with it all? I haven't seen nearly as many quilts come out of your house as I've seen bags of fabric go in."

"It's called stash, Sophie. If you'd agree to let me teach you how to quilt, you'd understand. Stash is critical. In fact, it's been said that whoever dies leaving the largest stash – wins."

"Wins?" Sophie responded sounding perplexed.

38

"Don't ask," Sarah said quickly, anticipating the next question

While they were out, they stopped at Ciara's for lunch and discussed the New Year's Eve party. Sarah described the plans she'd made with the caterer and told Sophie who was coming. "I wish Tim would be home by then," Sophie said regretfully.

"I'm sorry he'll be missing the holidays, but he'll be here in just a few weeks," Sarah reassured her friend.

"Let's hope I'm not in the state penitentiary when he gets here," Sophie muttered.

"Sophie! Don't be ridiculous. Have you heard from Officer Reilly?"

"No, not a word." Sophie looked hesitant and then added, "Do you think Charles could check things out for me. I know it's crazy, but I keep expecting them to come crashing through my front door with battering rams and machine guns."

"You're right about one thing – that is crazy. Sophie, they don't think you killed the man. Officer Reilly is just doing what he has to do – asking questions, getting the whole story down for the record. We'll know more once the medical examiner determines cause of death. Officer Reilly was probably right in the first place when he said the man died of natural causes."

"I guess you're right..." Sophie responded doubtfully, "but will you ask Charles to talk to them?"

Chapter 6

It was an exceptionally cold December morning as Sarah looked out the window at Barney who was making a quick trip to his spot at the back of the yard. She was glad they didn't have plans today. *It's a perfect day to stay in and sew*, she thought.

When the phone rang, she dried her hands on the kitchen towel and picked it up. "Sophie, slow down. What's happened?" When Sophie was excited her words came out in gusts making them hard to understand.

"It's Emma. She's gone."

"What do you mean?"

"Kelly called this morning to tell me that Emma never came back in after she let her out last night. She's been gone all night. I'm so worried, Sarah. What do you think happened to her? I never should have left her..."

"Sophie, you had no choice. You were doing your job. Do you suppose she's trying to get back to the cabin?"

"I hadn't thought of that. You may be right..."

"Do you want us to pick you up and drive out there just to see?"

"Yes, Sarah. Let's do it. Now that you mention it, I think that's exactly where she went."

Sarah sighed as she went into the sewing room and turned off the machine and the lights. "So much for sewing," she muttered.

"What?" Charles called from his den next door.

Sarah told him about Sophie's call and what they planned.

"I'd like to go with you if it's okay with you girls."

"We were counting on it," Sarah responded. "By the way, did you reach Officer Reilly this morning?"

"He wasn't in but I went ahead and called the medical examiner directly. I spoke with her assistant, and he told me the cause of death has been officially determined to be from natural causes."

"Natural causes?" Sarah responded looking baffled

"They found evidence of cardiac arrest. He had a massive heart attack."

"What about the blood?"

"He explained that the head injury occurred when he hit the floor.

"Does this mean they won't be investigating?"

"They'll write up their reports and close the case," Charles responded frowning.

"You don't look pleased."

"I'm pleased for Sophie. I know she's been worried, although she really didn't have anything to worry about. They weren't seriously considering her. My concern is simply that the poor guy isn't getting a fair shake."

"What do you mean?"

Charles sighed. "I don't really know what I mean. It's just that I haven't felt right about this case from the minute we walked into that cabin and were told it wasn't a crime scene. It didn't feel right then and it doesn't feel right now. Something more is going on here. I just think the case deserves a closer look."

"You think he was murdered?" Sarah asked.

"I think he might have been, but we'll never know. And if he was, the killer will go scot-free."

"What do you want to do?"

Charles was quiet as he contemplated his alternatives. "I think I want to look around. I don't know what I'm looking for and maybe nothing but I won't rest until I take a look."

"Then you have to follow those instincts, Charles. It's who you are."

Charles pulled her to his chest and held her close. "Thank you for understanding."

Gently pulling away, Sarah looked up at her husband with a twinkle in her eyes and said excitedly, "So, since we'll be out there anyway, how about we do some snooping on our own today?"

"My thoughts exactly. I'll grab my coat," Charles responded turning off his computer. Something out there had bothered him that night. He wasn't sure what, but he had a feeling that something was being missed. He knew the local cops didn't want to waste time on something they felt was not a crime. Yet Charles had continued to wonder.

"I'll warm up the car," Charles said pulling on his heavy jacket.

"I'll call Sophie and tell her we're on our way."

Sophie had little to say when she got into the car. She was clearly worried about Emma. "Do you think she'll be out there? It's so far and in this weather..." Her voice cracked as she tried to hide her apprehension.

"We'll find her," Sarah assured her friend. "In the meantime, we have some good news for you, Sophie," Sarah began, reaching back and taking her friend's hand. "They've determined the old man's death to be from natural causes."

"Does that mean they're stopping the investigation?"

Charles spoke up saying, "They'll close the case and that'll be the end of it."

"Do you suppose that man Reilly will call and apologize?" Sophie asked.

"I wouldn't hold my breath," Charles responded. "But it's over. You can relax."

"And I can leave town?"

"You're planning to leave town?" Sarah responded with surprise.

"No, I just don't like being told I can't." Sophie settled back into her seat with a long sigh and appeared to be lost in her own thoughts for the rest of the trip.

Charles was also quiet as he drove toward the cabin. He thought it was unlikely that the dog would be there, but he was glad for an opportunity to look around. He felt there was more to this case than met the eye. He had even wondered if there could be a connection between the Hawkins case and the case on the east side where he'd been questioning the neighbors. That case also involved an elderly man. Of course, in that case there was no question the man was murdered, and brutally so.

As they were approaching the cabin, Sarah broke his concentration by saying, "You're very quiet today." She reached over and touched the deep furrows between his brows as he drove. "What's bothering you?"

"Sorry. I was just thinking about work. Now, remind me where to turn," he said smiling and changing the subject.

You can't fool me, she thought, but decided not to pursue it. She knew he would tell her in his own time.

"Turn right here," Sarah said, pointing to the gravel road that led up the wooded ridge.

"I didn't notice those other log cabins when we were here before," Sophie comments from the back seat.

"There was an old, weathered sign back there that said this is Timberlake Village," Sarah responded. "It said something under that but I didn't see it in time."

Charles spoke up answering their question. "It said that this is a private lakeside community, but I don't see a lake and it's pretty run down. It may have been exclusive in its day, but not now.

"I wonder if we're supposed to be driving in without permission," Sophie asked.

Charles pointed out that there'd been no barriers or signs limiting visitors. "We're fine. Besides we have a mission."

They turned onto the road that lead up to Earl Hawkins' cabin and were surprised to see a car parked out front. "Someone's here," Sophie exclaimed.

"Maybe it's the guy's family," Charles responded. "You two wait here. I'll go up and ask about the dog. Maybe I can find out what's going on."

"Be careful," Sarah said before thinking.

Charles looked back at her and shook his head with a look of mild vexation. "I've been at this for many years, my dear. I'll be fine."

When a man stepped out on the porch pointing a shotgun, Charles stopped in his tracks and Sarah gasped. Sophie, on the other hand, jerked her door open and got out yelling, "Is that any way to treat guests? What's the matter with you? Put that gun down," and she proceeded to march up to the porch still talking to the man as if he were a misbehaving child.

Fortunately, the man actually lowered the gun, still resting his hand on the stock. "What do you want?" he demanded.

"That's more like it." Sophie introduced herself and went on to explain about the dog that was missing.

"My grandpa's dog?"

"Your grandfather?" she responded with surprise.

The man said he was Travis Hawkins, the grandson of the cabin's owner.

"I'm sorry about your grandfather," Sophie said and went on to tell him about her relationship to the dog and why she was there.

"You must be the lady that found grandpa? The police told me about you. Who are those other people out there?"

"They're my friends. They were here that night too." She turned and called to them. "Sarah, Charles, come on up and meet Travis Hawkins." She didn't mention that Charles was a retired detective. She didn't know why, but she felt that fact didn't need to be shared just now. Besides, she had already defined herself as the heavy in the group.

"Come on in," the man said once Charles and Sarah reached the porch. "I'm sorry about the shotgun. I'm from the mountains and I'm used to being cautious of strangers."

"Where about?" Charles asked.

"West Virginia. When they called me about grandpa, I drove on out. Someone needs to take care of his stuff and, I guess, sell the cabin. There's no other family, so I suppose that's me." He walked into the open kitchen and reached for a bottle of whiskey. "You folks want a drink? Grandpa's got glasses around here somewhere..."

"No thanks, Charles responded quickly. "How long had your grandfather been living out here?"

"Not sure. We haven't been in touch much. Let's see, I was about ten when he left I think so that'd be around twenty-five years ago. He moved out here with his wife.

"Your grandmother?"

"No, Granny died when I was a kid. I'm talking about his second wife, Rita. She was a pretty young thing. She wanted to leave West Virginia and move out here near her family. I heard she ran off or died or something."

"Did the police talk to you about how your grandfather died?" Charles asked.

"Probably old age, they said." He took a hearty gulp of his whiskey, nearly emptying the glass.

They sat and talked for a while about the community. It was Travis' first time there so he couldn't answer any of their questions. When asked about the lake, he responded, "Yeah, it's right up the road. In fact, the backside of this property runs right up to it. There's a couple of boats tied up down there.

Looks like a great place for fishin'." Hawkins added, "I looked around here for a rod, but I guess grandpa wasn't into that anymore. We used to fish back home when I was a kid."

"Your grandfather must have a sizeable lot here..." Charles commented.

"Yeah, looks like all these lots are ten or more acres, mostly wooded."

Charles asked to use the bathroom and Sarah figured he was using the opportunity to look around, although she figured they could see most of the cabin from where they were sitting.

When Charles returned, Travis poured himself another drink but didn't sit back down. Charles took the hint and said, "I think we'll be on our way." He took a business card from his wallet and handed it to Travis.

"A cop?" Travis Hawkins said looking surprised.

"Retired," Charles replied without explaining why he still had business cards. "Would you give us a call if the dog shows up here?" He then looked at Travis and added, "Unless you're planning to keep her yourself, of course."

"No way," Hawkins responded emphatically. "I've got a pack of dogs back home and sure don't want any more. I'll call you if I see it. What's this dog look like anyway?"

Sophie spoke up and told Hawkins that the dog was about thirty pounds, mostly white, and a bit straggly looking. "Oh and she has a pretty tail that curls up over her back. She's just a mutt but with a good scrubbing and a haircut she'd be quite a looker."

Hawkins chuckled and shook his head, obviously not accustomed to thinking of dogs that way. "A looker, you say?"

As they were walking out to the car, Sophie spotted Emma peeking out of the bushes just to the side of the driveway. "Emma," she said gently stooping down and holding out her arms. "Come here Emma."

The dog slowly approached her. "Hello girl. Did you walk all the way here?" The dog was panting and her tongue hung out from thirst.

Hawkins strolled toward them and the dog cowered and whined. "That must be grandpa's dog there," he said backing away.

Charles opened the door to the back seat and guided Sophie to her seat. He then turned to the dog and motioned for her to hop in with Sophie. Emma quickly jumped into the backseat and pressed her body against Sophie who wrapped her arm around the dog protectively.

Once they drove away, Sophie pulled out her cell phone and called Kelly at the farm to let her know Emma had been found. "Kelly, I'm going to take her home with me and talk to the Humane Society tomorrow to see if I can foster her at my house. She's really frightened and upset. I think she feels safe with me."

"Good idea, Sophie. Let me know how it goes."

Sophie moved over on the seat giving Emma lots of room. The dog stretched out and rested her head on Sophie's lap. "This pup has had a very rough week," she said, gently rubbing Emma's head as the dog sighed and began to relax.

Sarah looked back at the two and realized that both Sophie and Emma appeared to be at peace. "She's pretty dirty, Sophie. Would you like to bring her by the house and give her a bath in our utility tub? I bathe Barney there, and it's all set up with shampoo and towels."

"I'd like that," Sophie replied. "She needs to go to a groomer eventually, but a bath will be good for now. Maybe a good brushing too when we get home," she added running her hand through the dog's tangled fur. "Pull into that fast food place up there so I can get her some water and a hamburger."

Sarah and Charles shared a knowing glance and smiled. "I think our Sophie has herself a dog," Charles said softly.

* * *

"I had an interesting talk with the zoning commissioner this morning," Charles announced as he sat down to lunch a few days later. Sarah had all the ingredients for tacos spread out on the table and had called Sophie to join them.

"Tell us all about it," Sophie said as she piled chopped tomatoes, onions, and olives on the meat sauce that she had already scooped into her taco shell. She followed this with a handful of shredded lettuce and asked for a dollop of sour cream. "What's a dollop anyway," she asked before Charles could start talking.

"It's a small amount," Sarah responded.

"Then what I really want are several dollops please." Once her taco was ready to eat, despite half of it squishing out the sides and falling back on her plate, on her lap, and on the floor, she said, "Okay, tell us about the zoning commissioner." Barney, moving a little faster than usual, scarfed up what was on the floor beneath Sophie's chair and looked at what was on her lap with anticipation.

Sarah joined them at the table and began building her taco, which turned out to be much more manageable than Sophie's. "Why were you there?" Sarah asked, adding another question to the mix.

"Let me start from the beginning, and I'll answer both of your questions," Charles said, wiping the sauce from his chin. "Remember the last time we went out to Hawkins' place and we were intrigued by the sign, Timberlake Village? Well, I decided to talk to an acquaintance of mine who works for the county."

"Why?" Sarah asked, not following his thinking.

"I wanted to know more about the development and I'm not sure why – just a hunch, I guess."

"Was your friend able to help?"

"Well, he sent me over to see the zoning commissioner because he said that guy could give me the straight scoop. My contact admitted that most of what he knew was just hearsay."

48

"So what did you learn?" Sarah was getting interested and even Sophie had laid down her taco to listen.

"A man named Joseph Kirkland has submitted tentative plans for a 1200-acre resort and convention center on that land. He owns 300 acres of land adjoining Timberlake and has been buying out the current residents over the past couple of years. He now owns all the lots except the Hawkins place."

"Interesting…" Sarah mused. "Do you think…"

"Wait. Let me finish. The commissioner, his name is Anderson, pulled out the plans and let me look at them. There's a championship golf course, indoor and outdoor pools, a resort hotel with an upscale restaurant, cabins, a spa, and all the amenities. And then there's the convention center that will bring in business from all over the country. This is a multi-million dollar project."

"Our new acquaintance from West Virginia is about to become a very rich man himself," Sarah suggested.

"Oh, that's not the half of it. The resort hotel will be located on the Hawkins property overlooking the lake, and old man Hawkins was the only holdout."

"Do you suppose his grandson knows about this?" Sophie asked.

"Oh, I have no doubt about that," Charles replied.

Chapter 7

"Where are you two going?" Charles asked, looking at his wife who was bundled up in her long down coat and Barney who was now wearing an argyle sweater and was looking embarrassed.

"We've been invited for coffee and dog treats at Sophie's. We're going to introduce the dogs."

"That's right! They haven't met yet. This should be interesting."

"Do you want to come along?"

"No, I'll leave this experience to you two. I've got reports to type up for the department – never my favorite part of police work. At least now I can do them from home on the computer."

Sarah kissed his cheek and she and Barney headed for the door. "Oh, just a minute," he called out to her. "I have one more question. When do you want to put the tree up? I was thinking about bringing the boxes in from the garage this afternoon."

"I've been thinking about that too. Why don't we wait until the very last minute – like maybe the day of Christmas Eve? That way, the tree will still be fresh for the party on New Year's Eve."

"You want the tree up for the party?"

"I think it would be more festive, don't you?" she responded.

"Yes I agree, and that will give me some free time this afternoon. After I finish my reports, I think I'll go poke around Timberlake. I'm curious about the lake and its proximity to the Hawkins property."

Sarah had her mouth ready to warn her husband to be careful but remembered that he had seemed insulted by her lack of confidence in him the last time she had offered such a warning. Instead she smiled and said, "Have a good morning. We'll be back in a few hours."

Charles threw her a kiss as she went out the kitchen door. When he didn't hear the car start up, he looked out and saw the two trudging through the snow toward Sophie's house. He chuckled when he saw Sarah unclip Barney's leash and set him free to run with abandon through the drifts. *I guess his medications are working*, Charles thought with a smile.

It took them almost a half hour to reach Sophie's house what with all the detours Barney had to make in order to get the most out of being off leash. They were both covered with snow when Sophie opened the door.

Emma entered the foyer cautiously and looked at Barney. Barney wagged his tail. The two dogs cautiously performed the traditional sniffing rituals that all dogs perform as they get to know one another.

Sophie had coffee ready and invited Sarah to join her in the kitchen where she had a plate of breakfast muffins spread out along with butter, several varieties of jam, and a plate of assorted dog biscuits.

Both dogs followed them into the kitchen while eyeing one another guardedly. They made a few gestures seemingly to determine pecking order, but both being middle-aged in dog years apparently decided it wasn't worth the effort and they went to opposite sides of the room, sighed, and stretched out on the floor. Barney had clearly worn himself out romping to Sophie's house and Emma seemed to respect his condition.

"So tell me how it's going with Emma," Sarah said.

"We're doing just fine. She's on the relaxed side like I am. We both move around leisurely and we manage just fine. I had Caitlyn coming by to walk her, but she told me Emma starts looking back at the house by the time she gets to the end of the block, so I decided to just send her out back on her own."

Sophie had a fenced yard, which she rarely used and Sarah was glad to hear Emma was enjoying it. "By the way," Sophie added looking triumphant, "I was able to get an appointment with that fancy groomer downtown. You know, the one that was written up in the paper because some Hollywood producer flew him to California to groom the dogs in his movie."

"Today?"

"No, in a couple of weeks. I ordered their total beautification package," Sophie added with a mischievous grin as she poured two cups of coffee and set them on the table next to the tray of muffins.

"I've been thinking about something, Sophie. You said that these rescue organizations need money and I was wondering if they might like to run a raffle. If you like the idea, I was thinking about talking to the Friday Night Quilters. We could make a quilt and donate it to them as a fundraiser."

"Yes, that's a good idea," Sophie responded tentatively.

"You sound hesitant…?"

"No, it's not that. I love the idea. I was just thinking how much I'd enjoy being a part of that, but you know me. I can't thread a needle, much less make a quilt."

"You realize it's all done on the machine now, don't you?" Sarah asked.

"There's still a needle to thread…"

"How about if I were to promise to always thread your needle for you. Would you consider giving it a try?"

"Maybe…" Sophie responded thoughtfully. "Maybe."

Chapter 8

The doorbell chimed.

It was eight o'clock on New Year's Eve and the Parker house was brimming with friends and family. Sarah's son, Jason, was in the kitchen helping Sarah refill the platters while his wife, Jennifer, sat at the table holding their two-year-old daughter, Alaina, who was eating a peanut butter sandwich.

Martha, Sarah's daughter, was in the living room visiting with Andy and Sophie who had pulled up chairs near the refreshment table and were sampling the hors d'oeuvres.

The doorbell chimed again.

"Would you get the door, Charles?"

"I'm on my way," Charles called to his wife as he made his way through the crowded living room. "Good to see you, Andy," he said as he passed his neighbor and friend. "Is Caitlyn with you?"

"She's in the guest room playing with Barney," Andy responded just as Charles reached the front door.

Charles swung the door open and stood speechless. "John?" They hugged the way only a father and son can hug. There were tears in both men's eyes. "John, I had no idea you were coming."

"You weren't supposed to know. Sarah and I planned this surprise on our own. And that's only half of the surprise. Look who else is here," and he pulled his brother into the light. Charles hadn't seen his son, David, for many years and the two men were obviously at a loss as to how to break the ice. Finally David extended his hand and said, "Hi, Pop. Good to see you," and they shook hands somewhat awkwardly.

"Come in, come in," Charles said guiding his sons into the living room. "Friends, I want you to meet my sons. Some of you know John already, and this is his brother David."

"Hello all," David said as he closed the door. "Which one of you is the incredible Sarah my brother keeps talking about?"

Sarah stepped out of the kitchen and met David halfway across the living room. "So good to finally meet you in person, David," she said as she accepted his bear hug. He reminded her of a young Charles. "I'm so glad you agreed to come," she whispered to him.

"It was time," David responded. "It was time." They smiled at each other, both glad that she had called him. David and his father had been unnecessarily estranged since his high school years. Even talking to him on the phone, Sarah had felt he was ready to face his father and his own feelings. Seeing them together, she knew she had done the right thing.

"Did you fly in today?" Charles asked, taking their coats. Only Sarah noticed that his hands were shaking.

"Yes, we got here early this afternoon, checked into the motel, and spent the rest of the day checking out your delightful town."

"You should have stayed here with us..." Charles objected, but John interrupted him.

"I've already had that argument with your wife, Dad. We're fine right where we are. Now, take me to the food."

After filling their plates, the two brothers circulated around the house meeting and talking with the Parker's friends and Sarah's family. By midnight, the crowd was down to only ten. Jason and Jenny tried to get Alaina to sleep in the master bedroom, but she was wound up and fussy, so they decided to take her home. Several of the older folks left around eleven, but Sophie decided she would stay until the end. They got comfortable in the living room where they sipped wine and shared thoughts about the past year until the crystal ball dropped on Times Square.

Sophie got a ride home with Andy and Caitlyn, leaving John and David as the last to leave. Charles, catching David alone in the kitchen, put his hand on his son's shoulder and gentle spoke. "David, I'm sorry about everything. I know you got a raw deal when it comes to fathers…"

"Don't Dad. We've both made mistakes and we've both done the best we could with the hands we were dealt. I'm sorry about the part I've played in all this, but let's start fresh with this new year." He offered his hand and the two men shook. Charles couldn't resist, however, pulling his son into a hug.

After everyone had left, Charles reached into his pocket and pulled out a small box wrapped in gold foil. "Happy Anniversary, my dear," he said as he handed her the gift.

Later as Sarah was getting ready for bed, she looked in the mirror at the dainty gold chain and heart-shaped locket Charles had clasped around her neck. The locket was engraved with tiny flowers and inside he had placed a picture taken at their wedding. Sarah remembered that moment and loved that Charles understood what it meant to her. It was their first kiss as a married couple.

* * *

"Was that John on the phone?" Sarah asked as she poured her husband's coffee.

"Yes, actually both boys were on the phone." Sarah smiled hearing his fifty-something year old sons being called boys. "They'll be here in about twenty minutes." The night before, Sarah had invited John and David to come for breakfast, forgetting that the house was in disarray following the party. She and Charles got up early and together had the house in order and breakfast made before they arrived.

Sarah checked the casserole and saw that it would be done just in time. "That smells great," Charles said when the aroma wafted across the kitchen when the oven door was opened. "What's in it?"

"It's got all good stuff," she responded. "Sausage, cheese, sour cream, eggs, mushrooms, even some spinach for good measure."

"And this is on my heart-healthy diet?" he asked, already knowing the answer.

"One helping, my dear husband. Only one helping along with a couple pieces of dry toast to fill you up."

Charles grumbled but appreciated his wife's efforts to keep him on the straight and narrow after his recent stroke. "Just be thankful," she added, "that you're getting any of it at all."

When John and David arrived, Barney hurried to the door to greet them. "So this is the infamous dog that wouldn't come out of his room last night," David said, scratching Barney's ears until his eyes began to close. "And the cat? Where's she?"

Sarah pointed to the top of the kitchen cabinet above the refrigerator. "She's been there since the first guest arrived last night. She doesn't like for her peace and quiet to be disturbed."

Sarah pulled the casserole and biscuits out of the oven and placed them on the table, which was already set for four. They were all surprisingly hungry considering the amount of food that had been consumed the previous night.

Sarah accepted their praise as gracefully as she could considering she was pretty proud of the meal herself. She didn't often try out new recipes on guests but couldn't resist this one when she found it online.

"More casserole, Dad?" John asked passing the dish.

Charles glanced at Sarah and then answered, "No thanks, son. I'm fine."

"Am I missing something here?" John asked looking back and forth between the two. Sarah saw the slightest movement of Charles head indicating that she shouldn't respond. She immediately realized he hadn't told John about his stroke.

"Your father's on a diet," she responded with a half-truth.

John laughed and patted his father's stomach. "Getting a little flabby there, Pops?" he teased.

Charles gave Sarah a grateful nod and she silently vowed to talk with him about the importance of sharing his life with his sons, the good *and* the bad.

"So what do you boys want to do today?" Charles knew they had an evening flight.

"I'd like to just hang out and watch the game, if it's okay with you folks," John responded. "I have a case I was hoping to discuss with you, Dad, and I wanted to hear what you've been working on."

"Good idea," Charles responded. "David and I have lots of catching up to do too so let's stay around here, and later we can go out to dinner and we'll drive you to the airport in Hamilton."

"We have a rental car…"

"Let's turn it in here in Middletown. We can drive to Hamilton for dinner later. There are some great restaurants out near the airport."

The men took their coffee into the living room and turned on the game. Sarah smiled, happy to see Charles enjoying time with his sons. She decided to take Barney and walk down to Sophie's house, leaving the men to bond male-style – around a ballgame.

Chapter 9

"So what do you think?" Sarah had just told the Friday Night Quilters about her idea for a pet rescue fund-raising project and they were listening intently. The group of a dozen or so women had been meeting in the Running Stitches quilt shop since the week it opened, and Sarah had been a member since she moved to Cunningham Village. In fact, it was in this shop and with the help of these women that she had learned to quilt.

"I not only love the idea," Kimberly said, looking at her sister, "but we'll volunteer to quilt it." Her sister Christina enthusiastically nodded her agreement. The sisters, both in their late sixties, were original members of the Friday Night Quilters and had purchased a long-arm quilting machine the previous year. In addition to their own quilting, they offered their services to other members of the group for a nominal fee. "...and no charge for this one!" Kimberly added.

Ruth, the shop owner, offered to supply all the fabric for the project. They spent the rest of the meeting looking through pattern books and talking about what size to make the quilt as well as what pattern to use. They ended up with so many ideas that they decided to each go home and work up a suggested pattern and the group would vote on them the following week.

Sarah hurried back to Cunningham Village eager to tell Sophie about the meeting. She put in a quick call to Charles saying she would be late and then called Sophie to ask if it was too late to stop by. The meeting had run late, but she was eager to tell Sophie about it.

"Come on over, kid. I want to hear all about it." She put water into the coffee pot and filled the basket with decaf, knowing that Sarah couldn't handle caffeine in the evening. She laid out a plate of assorted cookies and was reaching for the sugar bowl when she heard Sarah at the door. "Come in," she yelled. "It's open."

"You know what Charles would say about that unlocked door," Sarah said as she pulled off her scarf and boots. Sophie handed her the knit booties she kept in a basket near the door especially for Sarah who always insisted on removing her shoes when she came in.

"Nonsense," Sophie grumbled. "That door hasn't been locked for ten years. I don't even know if I own a key."

"But Sophie..."

"I pay plenty for that security force sleeping in the entry kiosk. Let them do their job."

Sensing that Sophie was in a mood, Sarah remained quiet until Sophie had devoured two or three cookies. Sugar always sweetened her disposition.

"So tell me about the meeting. Did they like the idea?"

As Sarah talked about the quilter's response to their idea, Sophie grabbed a pad of paper so the two could start making plans.

"I think we should start with a small quilt like the one you gave me for my couch," Sophie suggested. Emma stood up and stepped out of her new fleece-lined dog bed which completed her collection. She now had one in every room. She walked across the kitchen floor and stretched out on the floor, resting her head on Sophie's foot. Sophie smiled and reached down to scratch her head.

"You mean a throw?" Sarah asked.

"Okay, if that's what you call it. I just think that would be a good way to test the waters and see if this can make a few dollars."

"Good idea," Sarah responded. "We can do a bed quilt sometime in the future if it seems worthwhile. That would be lots more work and much more expense."

Sarah reached for the pad and sketched out a couple of patterns that the group had considered earlier, but they couldn't come up with a way to relate the quilt block to the idea of rescued dogs.

Finally Sarah sketched a log cabin saying, "This is one of my favorite blocks."

Sophie looked at it and tilted her head thoughtfully. She pointed to the center block and asked, "Could that center be made bigger?"

"Sure. What do you have in mind?"

"Well, I was wondering...do they make fabric with dog designs on it?"

"Sure, all kinds – big dogs, small dogs, realistic ones, artsy ones, different breeds. Why?"

"Wouldn't it be cute to put a dog in the middle? It would almost look like it was in a dog house."

"Hmm," Sarah responded thoughtfully as she picked up the pencil. "We could make the center larger like this and add narrow strips around it." She quickly sketched a simple dog shape inside a larger center square and surrounded it with log cabin strips. "What about that?"

"Hmm," Sophie responded, cocking her head to the left. "Something's wrong." After a couple of moments, she brightened up and announced, "It needs a roof."

Sarah made a few adjustments to her drawing but suddenly squealed, "I've got it!" She turned to a fresh page and drew an elongated five-sided shape. "We'll modify the log cabin block to have five sides instead of four like this." She sketched a few logs all the way around and highlighted the two on the top that came to a point. "That's the roof," she added as she sat back to admire her work.

"A dog house -- I love it." Sophie reached for the pad and looked at it. "Would the quilt just be one great big dog house?" she asked. Not being a quilter herself, she wasn't sure how their design would be turned into a quilt.

"No, I'll suggest we make lots of these blocks and put them together with fabric strips between them. Everyone in the club could make a few dog house blocks."

Sophie sighed. "I'm sorry now that I was so stubborn last year when you wanted me to take your beginning quilting class," she said regretfully. "I'd really like to be a part of this."

"You can," Sarah said warmly, putting her hand on her friend's arm. "You could come to the club and help. Even if you don't want to sew, we need people for cutting and ironing. We'd love having you there...*I'd* love having you there. Will you consider it?"

"I just might," Sophie said with a half smile.

Chapter 10

Sophie woke up slowly, enjoying the comfort of the cozy quilt Sarah gave her for Christmas and the warmth of her husband's body snuggled against her back. Suddenly her eyes shot wide open and she bellowed, "....but my husband is dead!"

Instantly Emma jumped to her feet and shook the sleep from her eyes.

"What are you doing in my bed?" Sophie demanded, finally realizing the dog had snuck into her bed and wormed her way into her dream.

Emma stood on the bed next to her and wagged her tail. Sophie reached for her ear and scratched it. "I guess you're used to sleeping with your human, aren't you? I'm not sure we're going to do that here. For now, let me remind you where your bed is." She stood up and Emma quickly hopped off the bed and looked where she was pointing. "See, that's your bed right there."

Emma crept across the floor and got into the soft fleecy circle, turned three times, and laid down. Without lifting her head, she looked up at Sophie through her eyebrows contritely. "That's a good dog," Sophie praised. "Now let's go get some breakfast."

The phone rang just as Sophie filled her mug with coffee and steamed milk. She answered and spoke briefly to her dentist's office who had called to remind her of her impending appointment. She had just disconnected and returned to the kitchen when it rang again.

"How's a person supposed to drink a cup of coffee around here?" she muttered as she searched for the phone. "Where did I put that darn thing?" Emma followed her back into the living room, jumping out of the way when she turned abruptly back toward the kitchen. Emma shadowed Sophie where ever she went in the house and cried mournfully whenever she left the house without her. She was determined not to lose another loved one.

"Hello?" she finally answered, finding the phone next to the coffee pot.

"Mom, it's Tim."

"Hello son. I hope you're calling to tell me you have your ticket and you'll be here any day now. Am I right?"

"You're partly right, Mom."

"Only partly? What else?"

"I'll be there the day after tomorrow…"

Sophie squealed before he could finish. "Thursday? Oh Tim, I can hardly wait to see you. Charles has repainted your room and I've…"

"Mom, there's more."

"More?" Sophie responded.

"I bought two tickets, and…"

"Two tickets? Timothy Clifton Ward, don't tell me you're bringing a girlfriend. That lovely girl is waiting here for you…"

"Mom, no, I'm not bringing a girlfriend, and when I'm really serious about someone, you'll be the first to know. Well, at least the second." he added with a nervous chuckle. He knew his mother was curious about his relationship with Sarah's daughter, but he and Martha had agreed not to rush into anything.

"So why two tickets," Sophie asked with a frown in her voice.

"I didn't want to talk to you about this on the phone, but it looks like there's no other way. Mom, do you remember my old girlfriend, Betsy?"

"She's the one that wanted you to move in with her in that isolated cabin out in the Alaskan wilderness, right?"

"Well, it wasn't quite that bad. Her parents lived off the grid and she moved to their cabin after they died. And yes, she wanted me to move in with her but, of course, I didn't."

"But that was a long time ago, Timmy. Why are we talking about her now?"

"Okay, here goes. Betsy called me a couple of months ago and asked me to come out to the cabin. When I got there she introduced me to her fourteen-year old daughter, Penny. Actually, it's Penelope. She's named for Betsy's mother. Anyway, after we visited awhile, Betsy sent Penny outside so we could talk."

"Yes?" Sophie responding as she waited for the other shoe to drop.

"Betsy had terrible news. She had a very advanced form of cancer. The doctors were only giving her a couple of months to live."

"Oh my and such a young woman," Sophie responded. "How is she?"

"Mom, she died last week."

"Oh my, Timmy, I'm so sorry. What about the child?"

"She's with me."

"I don't understand. Doesn't she have family?"

"Mom, are you sitting down?"

Sophie dropped down on the couch and responded, "I am now..."

There was a long silence before Timothy spoke. "She's my daughter."

"What?" Sophie screamed. "I can't believe you never told me about this."

"I didn't know, Mom. Betsy never told me. She and I broke up years ago and I had no idea she was pregnant at the time."

Sophie, rarely one to find herself speechless, sat with her mouth open. Timothy waited, giving his mother a chance to digest the news. He finally spoke up, saying, "Mom? Are you still there?"

The words came out so softly that Timothy could barely hear them. "I'm a grandmother?"

* * *

Sophie drove to the airport alone despite Sarah's insistence that she and Charles drive her there. She wanted to be alone when she met her son and her new granddaughter. She had intended to arrive as the plane landed and wait in the short-term parking lot, but in the end she decided to arrive early and meet them as close to their gate as Security would allow. As she got out of the car, she reached for her cane but tossed it back in the car muttering, "That's not the way I want to meet my granddaughter." She turned and attached the Pup Mobile magnetic sign to the side of the van. "There," she said with a self-assured smile. "That should make her see that I'm one cool grandma."

As it turned out, the plane was late. Sophie found a seat and called Sarah.

"I told you we should have gone with you," Sarah responded when Sophie told her about the delay.

"And that would have gotten the plane here sooner?"

"Of course not, but we'd be there to keep you company…"

"Exactly why I called," Sophie responded. "Keep me company. In fact, start by telling me what Martha is going to think about this turn of events."

"I have no idea," Sarah responded. "She's turning forty-five this year and certainly isn't too old to be a mother, especially of a teenager, but she's never talked about children and I truly have no idea how she'll respond. It's been torture having to keep this to myself. She knew right away I was keeping something from her."

"You didn't tell her, did you? You know Timmy wants to tell her in person. I think he's worried about it too."

"I can't blame him. This is really big."

"I know. It's been hard for him too. He's in his fifties and certainly didn't have plans to start a family, but he's a good man. He's gentle and thoughtful and I think he'll make a good father."

"I have no doubt about that, Sophie. I was telling Andy about Penny and we were wondering whether his daughter, Caitlyn, might want to help her get adjusted…"

"Oops, gotta go, Sarah. They just announced the plane's arrival. I'm going to make my way over to Baggage Pickup so I don't miss them."

"Okay, Sophie. Call me when you can and let me know how it goes."

As Sophie made her way to the baggage kiosk her heart was fluttering. Never in her seventy-some years had she ever thought of having a grandchild. Timothy had shown no interest in marriage until he met Martha and she knew they wouldn't be starting a family at their age. She found herself thinking in terms of an adorable little girl and had to remind herself that Penny was practically grown. She herself was married when she was just two years older than Penny.

She sat down near the kiosk where she had a clear vision of passengers entering from Alaskan Airline flights and found her mind wondering back to those early years of her marriage. "At that age I thought I was a grown up," she told herself almost aloud. And by the time she lost three babies, she probably was a grown up despite her young years. In her late twenties Timothy arrived – a healthy, robust boy who brought with him all the happiness she and his father could imagine. It nearly broke her heart when he announced at the young age of seventeen that he was going to Alaska to work on the pipeline. She thought he would get it out of his system, but here he was returning nearly forty years later.

At that moment she spotted her burly son towering over most of the other passengers. He was tall and broad and still bearded, although he had told her the previous week he was thinking about shaving it off for his new life. She stood and waved and his eyes twinkled with excitement when he saw her.

As he approached, Sophie spotted the frail looking child leaning into him as if she were trying to disappear. She had limp blond hair and appeared pale by comparison to her son's suntanned and weathered look.

"Mama," Timothy cried as he reached out to hold her. "We didn't expect you to come inside but I'm so glad you did."

They both turned to the young girl by his side. Tim reached down and placed his hand under her chin and gently lifted her head. "This is my mother, Penny. Your grandmother."

A quiver of a smile passed the child's lips but didn't reach her eyes. She dropped her head again but softly muttered, "I'm very glad to meet you, ma'am."

"I'm glad to meet you too, Penny," Sophie responded. She placed her arm gently across the child's shoulder but didn't insist on a hug. Her own mother used to say, "Hug your Aunt Alma, kiss your Uncle Fred," and she had always hated it. She swore as a young child she would never do that to her own children and she never did.

"Let's grab our bags and head on out of here," Timothy announced cheerfully. He hurried toward the kiosk with Penny hanging onto the tail of his jacket. Sophie sat back down fighting to keep the tears at bay. *The child has lost her mother, gained a father and a grandmother she didn't ask for, has left her home and everything familiar, and yet she could find the words, 'I'm very glad to meet you, ma'am.' It's going to be an uphill battle, but that young girl is going to make it just fine.*

Timothy took the wheel on the way home and Sophie sat in the back with Penny. She told them both about the Pup Mobile and what she had been doing. Penny eyes got big as she listened to the stories about the dogs and timidly asked a few questions. "You could ride along with me sometime if you'd like," Sophie told her. "Oh, and I have a surprise that neither one of you knows about."

"What's that, Mom?" Timothy called back to her without turning his head. "I haven't seen traffic like this since…well, since the last time I was here," he added. "It doesn't get like this back home."

Back home? She wondered if he would ever think of Middletown as home again.

"Mom? The surprise?"

"Oh. I have a dog. Well, I don't exactly have a dog, but there's a dog living at my house."

"What does that mean?" Timothy asked.

She told them the story of Emma but leaving out the part about the dead body. She told him she has been certified as a foster home for dogs and Emma is with her at least temporarily.

"What does it mean to be a foster home, and what do you mean by temporarily?" Timothy called back with a frown she couldn't see, but heard in his voice.

"Timothy, this is a good thing." She went on to explain about foster care and that she probably wouldn't be taking in more than one dog at a time. "Right now I'm just taking care of Emma until a permanent home can be found for her." She didn't add that she had just about decided that she would be that permanent home.

"It just seems like a lot for you to be taking on at your age, that and the driving…"

She wanted to tell him not to treat her like an old lady, but she didn't want to argue with him tonight and certainly not in front of Penny. Actually, she had surprised herself over the past months as she learned she could do much more than she realized. *I wonder what he'd say if he knew I was thinking about learning to quilt.*

Chapter 11

"And what do you suggest we do with this information?" Charles sat across the desk from Officer Reilly trying to behave like the concerned citizen that he was rather than the detective that outranked this police officer, which he was no longer.

"Officer Reilly, I'm simply bringing you some new information that I feel puts a different light on the conclusions the department seems to have reached. Charles knew that the case had been closed in light of the Medical Examiner's results. "The victim, Earl Hawkins," he continued, "was the only holdout in Timberlake Village. This Kirkland guy bought up all the other lots and the Hawkins' lot was critical to his plans."

"What's so special about the Hawkins' lot?" Reilly asked without much interest.

"It overlooked the lake. The Hawkins' lot was the planned location for the hotel and convention center."

"So the guy wouldn't sell. What's your point?"

If this is what our police department has come to, I'm glad I retired when I did. Charles attempted to smile and went on to explain. "It gives several people motive to kill the guy."

"Several?" Reilly repeated, looking up but remaining skeptical.

"Yes, several. Joseph Kirkland, the developer, for one. Hawkins' grandson for another. Any number of investors yet unknown. The list goes on." Charles sat quietly and watched the officer as he digested what Charles had said.

The officer finally spoke. "I'll talk it over with the lieutenant and see what he wants to do, but as far as I'm concerned, the case is closed and what you're suggesting is a huge waste of valuable time."

Reilly stood and walked out of the room. Charles assumed he had been dismissed and stood to leave as well. On his way through the lobby, Reilly yelled to him, "The lieutenant wants to see you." He had a cocky look on his face giving the impression he had won this round.

"Charlie, good to see you," the lieutenant said, standing and stretching his arm across the desk to shake Charles' hand. Everyone in the department had always called him Charlie despite his preference for his given name. Matthew Stokely had been Charles' immediate supervisor and was promoted to lieutenant just as Charles was retiring. Because of their special working relationship, Stokely had arranged for Charles to work for the department as a contractor from time to time when he was needed. Stokely had tremendous respect for Charles, both as a friend and as a detective.

"Reilly tells me you have some questions about the Hawkins case. Sit down and let's look at it. Coffee?" Charles said he'd take his chances on a cup and that he hoped it had improved over the years. "Not much," Stokely responded with a chuckle as he filled a mug and passed it to Charles. Sitting back down at his desk, Stokely opened the file folder Reilly had tossed on his desk and quickly reviewed the reports. "Tell me about your concerns," he said as he finished and closed the file.

Charles told him about his visit to the zoning commissioner and about the resort and convention center, which Joseph Kirkland was planning. He explained that Kirkland had managed to purchase all the homes in Timberlake Village with the exception of the Hawkins property.

"And you think Hawkins might have been murdered by this Kirkland guy?"

"I never said that, Matt. I don't know if he was murdered or not and there's a good chance the guy actually did die of natural causes. What I'm saying is that there's been no investigation. There are people with motives, yet the case was closed without looking at possible scenarios. That's all I'm saying."

"People with motives…" Matt reflected thoughtfully.

"Yes, for example the Kirkland guy. Or the grandson who will probably become a very rich man as a result of his grandfather's death. Or any number of other players we don't even know about because this case hasn't been investigated as a possible homicide," he added beginning to raise his voice slightly.

"Take it easy there, pal. Remember that ticker of yours." Not only had Stokely been his superior, but he and Charles had become close friends over the years. Stokely had seen Charles through the dark days after his wife's death and later spent hours with him in the hospital and the rehab facility following Charles' massive stroke.

Stokely pulled out a yellow pad and began taking notes. He asked for more details regarding the resort and the people Charles had spoken with. He laid his pen down and sat quietly for a while staring out the window, something Charles had learned over the years meant that the mental wheels were spinning. He picked up the case record again and reread Reilly's notes.

Matthew Stokely sighed and shook his head looking defeated. He had more cases on his desk than he could assign. Two men were out following injuries on the job and the mayor was on his back about two unsolved cases that had hit the newspapers.

"I can't assign this case right now, Charlie. Reilly and his team are working full time on the south side case and I don't have anyone else I can assign. I'm sorry. I agree it could use a closer look, but I just don't have the manpower."

The two men sat silently and finished off their now cold coffee. Stokely looked up at Charles and asked, "Do you have the time to take on a case?"

"You mean this one?"

"Yes."

"Sure, Matt. I can look into it."

"I wish I could give you an officer at least part time to help out, but it's not in the cards."

"Sarah can be my sidekick. She loves this sort of thing."

"Well, you two be careful and keep me in the loop, okay?"

"It's a deal," Charles responded as he stood and again shook hands with his old friend.

* * *

Sarah and Barney, both covered with snow, were just coming home from the park. She pulled off her boots and reached for a towel to dry the snow off Barney who was still leaping around with excitement. The phone rang while she was hanging up her coat. She reached for it with one hand still holding Barney's leash in an attempt to keep his wet feet off the rug. "Hello?"

"So Mother, you knew about all this?" Martha's voice was trembling with anger.

"I assume you mean about Penny," Sarah responded. "Martha, I've only known for a few days, and I wanted to tell you, but I promised Sophie I wouldn't."

"You promised *Sophie*?" her daughter said sarcastically. "Surely your alliance is to me, *your daughter*, before Sophie."

"Martha, you know how important it was for Timothy to tell you this himself. This was *his* news to tell, not mine."

"News? It's much more than *news*," her voice still laced with sarcasm.

"I'm sorry I had to keep it from you, Martha. Why don't you come over and have dinner so we can talk. I know you're upset."

"I don't want to come over there, and I don't want to talk." Martha hung up.

Sarah shook her head wishing her daughter could handle problems without first striking out at everyone within reach. She

72

finished drying the snow off Barney and followed him into the kitchen. After his outings he always felt entitled to a treat and he was usually right. He carried the biscuit across the kitchen to his mat and attempted to make room for himself next to Boots the cat who was sprawled out leaving little room for him.

The phone rang and Sarah smiled to see her daughter's name on the display. "Hi Martha," she answered calmly.

"I'd rather meet somewhere. Could we go to Tony's for pizza? Just the two of us?"

"Sounds fine. I'll see you there in a half hour."

Sarah arrived before Martha and found a table in the corner near the fireplace. She went ahead and ordered two glasses of wine and looked over the menu while watching the door.

When Martha came in Sarah was prepared for her to be angry, but instead she looked like she'd been crying. Sarah stood and Martha walked into her arms.

"I'm sorry, Mom. I didn't mean to jump all over you. I'm just so upset. I don't know what to do. I love Tim but I don't know if I can do this."

"Sit down, sweetheart, and take a sip of your wine. I've ordered us each a cup of minestrone while we decide what we'll have for dinner."

"What about Charles?" Martha asked.

"I told him we'd bring him a pizza."

Martha smiled and touched her mother's hand across the table. "I'm sorry I got so angry, Mom. I don't know what got into me; this isn't your fault."

"You're scared, honey. This is a very big thing. If you marry this man, you'll be an instant mother of a teenage child – a child with lots of baggage. Anyone would be upset."

"Upset, yes, but I was unfair to you. I really do understand why you couldn't tell me and I'm glad I heard it first from Timothy. I think he's as scared as I am. Neither one of us has any idea how to care for a child."

"Have you met her?"

"Not yet. Tim said she's shy and doesn't want to meet anyone yet, but he said his mother is getting along with her just fine. I guess the dog helps. Penny's crazy about Emma. Have you met the child?" Martha asked.

"No. Sophie told me the same thing. They're just letting her set the pace. She's really bonded with Sophie's dog though. Emma's been sleeping with Penny every night." Sarah smiled as she thought about how a dog can reach into a person's heart and ease the pain. "It's that unconditional love she's giving Penny, something she probably lost when she lost her mother."

"I don't know if I have that to give. You have it, but I don't think I do. Sometimes I can be so judgmental..."

"Honey, don't be so hard on yourself. You've travelled a hard road and have had to toughen up. But I know the softness is there. Remember, I knew you when you were growing up and there couldn't have been a more loving child. You have it in you; you just haven't had an opportunity to use it. At work, you're isolated in your laboratory and, until you met Tim, you haven't had much in the way of a personal life since the divorce. Just relax and let it come naturally."

"Assuming it ever will," she responded in a defeated tone. "I guess I'm a little afraid of the child, too. What if she doesn't like me? What if..."

"Martha, slow down. This probably isn't any of my business, but have you made a commitment to Timothy?"

"A commitment?"

"Have you agreed to marry him," she clarified bluntly.

"Oh. No, we enjoy being together and when we talk about the future, it includes both of us together, but we haven't actually verbalized it that way. I suppose we might have -- but now, I just don't know."

"So, what I'm saying, I guess, is you don't need to make a commitment to Penny either at this time. Just meet her. Go out with her and Tim. Maybe take her shopping. Just see where it goes. You don't have to like her and you don't have to marry Timothy. Just take it, as Andy says, "one day at a time."

When their meals arrived, they lapsed into lighter conversation with Sarah telling her daughter some of the outrageous tales Sophie told about her experiences in the Pup Mobile. "My guess is," she added with a chuckle, "that many of her stories are grossly exaggerated, but they're all fun to hear."

"If anyone can help that young girl adjust to her new life," Martha said thoughtfully, "it will be Sophie."

Chapter 12

"Good evening everyone," Ruth announced as she walked into the already filled classroom. She had just locked the door to the shop and was ready to relax with the Friday Night Quilters. She reached around the corner into the shop's kitchenette and brought out a platter of assorted cookies and placed it in the center of the large table the group had created by pushing four workstations together in the middle of the room. "Help yourselves to coffee or tea and let's get started. First of all, let's meet our guest. Sarah, would you tell us who you brought with you tonight?"

"I'd love to," Sarah responded with a big smile as she stood and turned to the woman sitting next to her. "This is my friend and neighbor, Sophie Ward. Sophie is the person responsible for this project. She volunteers with a pet transportation service called Sheila's Shuttle. She transports animals from shelters to foster homes or to their forever homes, and she is currently fostering a wonderful dog named Emma. Sophie told me about the need for funds in the animal rescue world and helped me to design our suggestion for a rescue quilt that can be raffled off as a fund raiser."

By this time Sophie was blushing and making dismissive hand gestures at Sarah. Everyone clapped and welcomed Sophie to the group.

"Sophie," Ruth said, "We're very happy to have you with us." Turning to the group, she added, "Let's all introduce ourselves. "Christina, will you start?"

"Sure," Christina responded. "I'm Christina and this is my sister, Kimberly. We've been in the club since the beginning. What has it been," she asked turning toward Ruth, "about ten years now?"

76

"We started the group right after I opened the shop, so yes, that was ten years ago," Ruth responded.

Since her sister had already introduced her, Kimberly simply said, "Glad to meet you, Sophie. I hope you keep coming."

Delores was sitting next to Kimberly and was the most experienced in the group. "Hi Sophie. We're all happy to have you join us. Actually, I met you last year in the shop at Ruth's anniversary party."

"I remember," Sophie responded with growing excitement. "You were serving that incredible chocolate cake – the one with the chocolate curls on top."

"Yes," Kimberly exclaimed. "You called it the Ultimate Chocolate Sin."

"I'd almost forgotten about that recipe," Delores responded. "Double cream, as I recall, mounds of dark chocolate, and a dreadful amount of sugar. Oh, and lots and lots of butter..."

"Ooh," the group moaned in unison.

"Okay," Ruth said laughing as she attempted to get the group back on track. "Let's get on with the introductions. Allison?"

"Hello Sophie. I'm Allison Bennett. I have an Aunt Sophia. Is that your real name?"

"Actually, it's not a nickname. My mother named me Sophie for one of her friends who was probably a Sophia, but my mother only knew her as Sophie."

Allison had a small pillow on her lap and was working on an applique project. She held the project up for the group to see. "I started this at our last meeting and it's almost finished. I'm hoping to have it framed for my sister in time for her birthday."

"It's beautiful," Sophie responded, squinting to see the detail. Allison carried it over to her so she could see it up close. "Really exquisite," Sophie added.

Allison sat back down and arranged her project across the pillow she held on her lap. "What's that little pillow for?" Sophie asked.

"It keeps my hands and elbows elevated so there's not as much stress on my neck and shoulders."

"Good idea," Sophie responded. "I think that would help me with my embroidery projects."

"It would, Sophie," Ruth offered. "I have a couple of lap pillows in the back if you'd like to look at them after the meeting."

"Thank you, Ruth. I'd like to see them." Looking at the next person, Sophie smiled and said, "And I already know this young lady. Hi Caitlyn." Caitlyn was Andy's sixteen year old daughter and the youngest member of the group. She had been coming to the meetings sporadically at first but had attended all the meetings for the last six months. Andy had told Sophie that his daughter really enjoyed being included and was spending more and more time sewing at home.

"Hi Sophie," Caitlyn responded. "I hope you keep coming. We have lots of fun."

"We do," the woman sitting next to Caitlyn added softly. "I'm Margaret, by the way." She dropped her eyes and didn't say anything else. Margaret had only been in the group for a few months and seemed extremely shy, although she had produced some extraordinary items.

Sensing Margaret's discomfort, Ruth moved on to the next person. "Jolene?"

"Hi, I'm Jolene and I can't wait to start looking at what people came up with for this rescue quilt." Jolene had moved to Middletown from a small town in Texas and everyone enjoyed the twang she brought with her. "Let's get this show on the road," she added eagerly. "Oh, and this is my friend Tessa. She helped me with my idea."

"Tessa, are you a quilter?" Ruth asked.

"No, I wouldn't know which end of the needle to thread," she hooted.

"I can relate to that," Sophie muttered just loud enough for Sarah to hear.

"I'm just here visiting Jolene," Tessa continued in a more serious tone. "I'm on my way back to Texas tomorrow."

"We're glad to have you with us," Ruth responded. "Okay Sophie, you've met most of the club. We have a few other members, but these are our regulars."

"By the way," Delores said, "Sophie, do you quilt?"

"No, but if my friend here keeps nagging at me about it, I might have to give up and learn how," she responded. Once the ice was broken, Sophie relaxed and began to entertain the group with her animal-transporting tales.

Finally Ruth spoke up saying, "Well Sophie, we're delighted that you came tonight and it's unlikely that we'll let you get away. You'll be quilting before you know it." Everyone clapped their encouragement. "Now," she added, "let's decide what our quilt will look like." Several of the members began pulling projects out of their tote bags. "I can hardly wait to see your ideas. Who wants to go first?"

No one volunteered, so Kimberly and her sister Christina stood up and walked over to the design wall. They had each made a block that they placed on the flannel wall. Kimberley had done a Duck and Ducklings block with a fussy-cut square in the middle surrounded by small Flying Geese blocks. Her sister did a Goose Tracks block. "We were thinking of a sampler quilt using blocks named for different animals. Everyone could choose a block to make and we could put them all together with sashing."

Delores who was the oldest person in the club and the most experienced spoke up saying, "That's a terrific idea, girls. There's the Fox and Geese block, Doves in the Window, Hens and Chicks, Flight of Swallows ..."

"How about the Bear's Paw?" Caitlyn called out. With Sarah's help, she had just completed a Bear's Paw quilt for her bed.

"That's a good one," Allison responded. "Most of the traditional blocks have to do with birds and wild animals, don't they? I can't think of any having to do with dogs or cats."

"Well, all types of animals need to be rescued at one time or another..."

"That's true, so how about the Buffalo Ridge..."

"...and the Money Wrench..."

The group, at this point, was giggling and tossing out names of blocks.

"Oh! Oh! I've got it," someone called out. "There's the Cat's Cradle and the Calico Puzzle."

"...and Puss in the Corner..."

"Excellent," Ruth said enthusiastically. "Okay, so we have one suggestion on the table. Does anyone else have another idea for our rescue quilt?

"Before we go on, I have a question about this one. People who don't know the names of quilt blocks won't realize our quilt has to do with animals."

"We could make a label for the back, which lists the names of each block."

"Great idea," Delores responded. "I have an embroidery machine and I could make the label."

"Excellent," Ruth exclaimed. "Now are there any other suggestions for a quilt design?"

"Mine is very simple," Margaret said quietly. "I was just thinking that we all have fabrics in our stash with pictures of animals. We could make a single Irish chain with a colorful nine patch block alternating with a fussy cut animal picture."

"That would be interesting," Delores commented. "The quilt would be covered with animal pictures with a chain going horizontally between them."

"I have a whole section of animal motifs here in the shop," Ruth offered. "That would indeed be interesting and very unusual. Anyone else?"

Jolene stood and tugged on Tessa sleeve, encouraging her to stand. "Come on," she said. "You promised to help." The two women stood by the design wall and Jolene pulled a block out of her tote bag. "Now this one is my dog." She went on to say that her husband had transferred the photograph onto white muslin. She had used the picture as the center of a Friendship Star block using colors that complemented her black and white border collie. "And Tessa..." she began, encouraging her friend to display the second block.

"This is my dog," Tessa announced as she placed the block on the design wall. "Jelly Bean is a corgi and he helps my husband on the ranch back home."

"Her husband fancies himself a rough and tumble cowboy," Jolene added giggling. Tessa shot her a look, indicating this was a long-standing private joke. "Show them the other one," Jolene encouraged.

"Okay, this one is my son's dog," and she added a pink friendship star block surrounding the picture of a tiny Chihuahua with a ribbon in her hair. She was proudly perched on the arm of a strapping soldier dressed in military fatigues. "Her name is Missy."

Everyone laughed. Sophie asked, "What does your cowboy think of his son's dog?"

"We don't discuss it," Tessa responded.

"So Jolene," Kimberly asked, "how did your husband get the pictures onto the fabric?"

"I know the answer to that," Sarah spoke up. "We did that at my mountain retreat last fall." She proceeded to describe the technique and Jolene volunteered her husband's services. Ruth added that she had the kits if anyone wanted to try it themselves.

"I don't have a dog," Allison remarked.

"Neither do we," Christina added.

"Perhaps we could take a field trip to the shelter and take pictures. That way we could say that some of the dogs on our quilt are waiting to be adopted."

"That's a good idea," Ruth added. "Also, we all have friends with dogs. I'm sure we can come up with enough pictures for a quilt. Any other comments about this one?"

No one spoke so Ruth asked if there were any other suggestions.

"My friend here has an idea," Sophie offered, wondering why Sarah hadn't spoken up.

"It's not just my idea," Sarah responded. "Sophie and I came up with this one together." She walked up to the design board carrying the pizza box that she used to transport completed quilt blocks. Sophie had once asked her if they didn't get greasy, but Sarah assured her she had gone to the pizza place for a clean box.

Sarah pulled out the first block she had made and placed it on the wall. The group responded with ooh's and ah's. The block was a five-sided Log Cabin block with a fabric in the center featuring a dog. The dog appeared to be sitting in a colorful dog house. She had added sky and grass fabrics to complete the block and had trimmed it to a rectangle.

She then placed a second one on the board. This one had two dogs in the dog house with a colorful sunset sky and flowers in the yard. The third one, she explained, was a Courthouse Steps block but was still five sided with the two upper blocks forming the roof. Everyone was talking at this point and clearly loved the design.

"I think this is the one we should do," someone called out. "It's adorable!"

"Let's vote on it," Ruth said as she ripped pages out of a small pad and passed them around. "But these are all good ideas, and I think we should make all of them if this turns out to be a good source of funds for the shelter. Write down your choice for this first one."

Once Ruth had all the folded sheets back, she opened them one by one and placed them all on one pile while everyone watched eagerly. "Okay, we have a winner," Ruth said beaming. "The winner is *Dog Houses by Sarah and Sophie.*" Everyone clapped their approval. "And I'd like to add that it was unanimous."

All speaking at once, the group talked about the animal fabrics they had in their stash. Once they settled down, Ruth asked Margaret, Kimberly, Jolene, and Christina to save their designs for their next rescue quilt. The group decided that the next meeting would be a work shop and everyone would bring a bag of brightly colored scraps and any dog fabric that had on hand.

"We'll look at what we have," Ruth said, "and fill in what we need with fabric from the shop. I'll provide the sashing, borders, and back along with any additional pieces we need. I'm hoping you ladies have some dog fabrics. I don't have much on hand."

"I have several yards of assorted dogs," Delores said. "I'd be happy to contribute that."

"I have an animal collection. I'll pull out the dogs," Allison offered.

"Did you have any of the fabric left over that you used for Barney's quilt?" Sophie asked turning to Sarah.

"Yes! And that has five or six different breeds on it. I'll pull that out."

"I think we're well on our way," Ruth said enthusiastically. "Next week we'll have a work shop and get started on our blocks. "It looks like we'll have enough dogs. Check your stash and see if you have any fabric with skies or trees for behind the dog houses."

"… and rocks or grass for the ground below," Sarah called out.

"Also flowers," Christina added. "Don't forget the flowers."

As Sarah and Sophie were leaving, Ruth said, "Oh, wait a second Sarah. I wanted to ask you about the five-sided center piece. Did you use a pattern for that piece? The three blocks you displayed seemed to be consistent sizes."

"Yes. I made a plastic template. I'll bring it next week. It's just five-sided with the two opposite sides being elongated to form the walls."

"Good. I'll use yours to cut templates for everyone. I'll see you next week and Sophie, promise me you'll be here."

"I'll be here," Sophie responded.

As they were driving home, Sarah turned to Sophie and said, "So honestly, what do you think of the group?"

"I think it would be worth learning to thread a needle if it meant I could be part of that group."

Sarah, knowing Sophie had been enjoying herself, smiled and said, "You already are a part of that group, my friend. You already are."

Sophie reached over and gave her friend's arm a quick pat.

* * *

"How was your meeting?" Charles asked as he reached for her pizza box so she could remove her coat and boots.

"Wonderful," she responded with a broad smile, "And Sophie loved it."

"She did?" he responded somewhat surprised. "And did they like the dog house design you gals worked up?"

"They sure did. They chose it for the rescue quilt," she announced proudly. "I think it's going to be really cute. We picked most of the fabrics and Sophie found a sashing fabric that's just perfect. It's black with colorful paw prints all over it.

We'll use it between the blocks and possibly for the border. Ruth is donating all the fabric for the project."

She hung up her coat and turned to continue talking to him about the meeting, but he was already heading toward the kitchen. "Coffee?" he asked.

"Decaffeinated," she responded.

"And how about a slice of carrot cake?"

"I'll skip that. I had a couple of cookies at the meeting."

"Well," he responded thoughtfully, "I'll have carrot cake. I didn't get my seven fruits and vegetables today."

"Just a minute..." she responded, pretending indignation. "Surely you haven't been counting carrot cake as a vegetable on your food diary."

"Of course I have," he teased. "Now tell me about your meeting."

"I'll get to that, but first I want to tell you about my talk with Caitlyn. During the break I sat down with her and told her about Penny."

"They haven't met?"

"Not yet. In fact, Penny hasn't met anyone yet and Sophie thinks it's time. She's going to have a small party for her next week...just a few of us along with Andy and Caitlyn."

"Where are they going to live? Here with Sophie?"

"The retirement village rules don't allow it."

"I hadn't thought about that. How is Caitlyn able to live here with Andy?"

"Remember, Andy filed for an exception. She's listed as his caregiver, although we both know Andy doesn't need any care. But Sophie couldn't do that for Timothy and Penny both. Actually, they need their own place anyway."

"True. It's going to be an adjustment for both of them, but it would be good if they could be close to Sophie."

"I agree. Tim is hoping to find something within walking distance of Cunningham Village."

"So back to your talk with Caitlyn," Charles said getting them back on topic. "What did Caitlyn have to say when you talked to her tonight?"

"She's a couple years older than Penny, but she offered to help her get acclimated. It's not clear whether they'll be in the same school. Penny was in the eighth grade when she left Alaska, but she'll have to be tested to determine her grade level."

"Why wouldn't she just go into eighth grade?"

"Well, her mother was home-schooling her and the school system needs to review her records and do grade-level testing. Tim is actually hoping she can go into the high school. It's right up the street and he's looking at an apartment complex just on the other side of the park."

"Also she'd be in the same school as Caitlyn, right?"

"Yes, Caitlyn's in the tenth grade, but they'd be in the same building. If she has to go to the middle school, she'll be catching a bus. I guess Tim is just hoping to reduce the number of changes in her life."

"I hope he doesn't go too far the other way. She doesn't need to be overprotected either," Charles responded.

"I don't think Sophie will let that happen."

"So when's this party?"

"Saturday. To keep it simple, Sophie's just doing lunch for you and me, Martha, Andy, and Caitlyn."

"Martha? Martha hasn't met her either?"

"No and they wanted to keep that introduction casual. She could easily rebel if she thinks she's being introduced to a new mother."

"I see," he responded frowning. "But actually…"

"I asked her, Charles. Martha said she and Tim haven't even discussed marriage. She wants to get to know Penny on her own before she makes a commitment to either one of them. Taking on a family at this point in her life is something she's just not sure she wants to do."

"Oh."

His tone reminded her of the tone he used when she, herself, was expressing her own reluctance to make a commitment. She hadn't thought about it before, but her daughter was much like she was about making major life changes. She too had balked at getting seriously involved with Charles.

"She's just being cautious," Sarah added.

"Like her mom," he responded without looking up.

"Yes, I guess 'like her mom.'"

After a short pause, he raised his head and asked, "Were you ever sorry?"

"Not for a minute," she answered with a twinkle in her eye, which he returned.

Chapter 13

Charles and Sarah were the first to arrive at Sophie's house on Saturday. Tim and Penny were sitting on the couch watching a quiz show. Tim immediately stood up, hugged Sarah warmly, and reached out to shake hands with Charles. "Good to see you folks again. It's been a long time. In fact, the last time I saw you two was at another party..."

"Our wedding," Charles replied with a broad smile. "Happiest night of my life," he added.

"You charmer," Sarah responded, lightly tapping him with her hand. Turning to the young girl on the couch, she said, "and this must be your daughter." She held out her hand, and Penny stood and shyly offered her own. "I'm Sarah Parker. If it's okay with your father, please call me Sarah." Penny looked toward her father who nodded his approval.

"Glad to meet you," Penny said softly. "I'm Penny."

"So glad to meet you, Penny. And this is my husband, Charles."

At that moment, Emma came bounding into the room.

"Oh my!" Sarah exclaimed, placing her hand on the side of her face. "She's beautiful."

Sophie turned the corner right behind Emma and beamed with pride. "Isn't she something? The groomer was delighted with what he found under that matted fur...a beautiful young lady!" Emma held her head and tail high and pranced around seeming to understand that all the fuss was about her.

"Barney should see her now. He'd be instantly in love."

"Let's hope not," Sophie said with a frown, forgetting that puppies were out of the question for either of their dogs.

About that time there was another knock at the door and Tim hurried to open it. An almost imperceptible look of disappointment crossed his face that only Sophie could see. It wasn't Martha.

"Andy, come on in. Is Caitlyn with you?"

"She'll be right along. She went back to change her outfit."

"To change?" Tim responded incredulously. "Why?"

"Oh, you have a lot to learn about these young girls of ours," Andy chuckled. "Just wait."

"Speaking of young girls, I'd like you to meet my daughter, Penelope." Penny frowned. "Oh, sorry. I mean my daughter, Penny."

"See? What did I tell you?" Andy said softly as an aside to Timothy. "Hi Penny. I'm very glad to meet you. My daughter, Caitlyn, will be along soon."

Penny smiled and said she was glad to meet him. "How old is Caitlyn?" she asked shyly.

"Caitlyn is sixteen. She's been with me for the past two years. Her mother died too," he responded and Penny immediately dropped her eyes. Sarah could see her body curl slightly forward as if she were a fading flower. "Oh, sorry," Andy added. "I guess I shouldn't have…anyway, Penny, I'm glad to meet you."

"Me too," she said without looking up.

"I'm going to leave you folks to visit," Sophie said. "Sarah, will you help me in the kitchen?"

Sarah stood to follow her just as there was another knock at the door. "Timmy," Sophie yelled. "Will you get that?"

Once in the kitchen, Sophie exclaimed, "It took me all morning to convince that young girl to come out of her room and meet people. It only took Andy one second to convince her it was a mistake."

"It's not that bad, Sophie. It's actually a good thing for Penny to know that she and Caitlyn share something very

89

fundamental. They've both lost their mother and they can be a support to one another."

"You're probably right," Sophie replied. "I keep telling Tim that he's being overprotective, and here I am doing it myself. Her mother *did* die. There's no reason to pretend it didn't happen, but we haven't mentioned it once since she got here."

"I think things will look up once she gets into school," Sarah said reassuringly.

"You may be right. Timmy met with the school counselor yesterday and they're starting testing this week to determine her grade level and any special needs she might have." After a short pause, Sophie said, "Would you peek around the corner and see who came in?"

"Oh, it's Martha. Martha, we're in here," she called to her daughter. She had to laugh to herself when she noticed that Tim and Martha were sitting on opposite sides of the room as if they were practically strangers.

"I'll be right in," Martha responded. As she stood, Martha turned to Penny and said, "Shall we go see if we can help with lunch?" Sarah saw Penny's eyes light up with appreciation that someone was getting her out of the fishbowl. Once they were in the kitchen, Martha immediately started getting dishes out and suggested Penny get the silverware.

"How many will we be?" Martha asked.

"Nine counting Emma," Sophie responded.

Martha and Penny gave each other a look and Martha said, "I guess that means eight of everything."

"Get one of the men in here to put a leaf in the table," Sophie added.

"Do you want to get your dad?" Martha asked Penny, and the young girl smiled and nodded.

"You're a natural," Sarah whispered to Martha. "And you thought you didn't have it."

90

Martha just smiled. "She reminds me of myself at that age," she said softly.

Once the table was set and they were shuffling around deciding who would sit where, the doorbell rang again and Emma ran to the door. "That would be Caitlyn," Andy said, and he headed for the door behind Emma.

After Andy introduced the girls and everyone was seated, Sophie opened the oven and pulled out a deep-dish lasagna and a tray of garlic bread. She placed them both on trivets on the table and went to the refrigerator. She returned with a gigantic bowl of colorful salad. "Dig in," she announced as she pulled out the chair at the head of the table and sat down.

Sarah noticed the salad included every vegetable she could imagine. In addition to the usual lettuce-tomato-onion medley, she saw slices of squash, cabbage, carrots, radishes, broccoli, and leaves of spinach, radicchio, and kale. And to top it off, she had included slices of apple along with strawberries and almond slivers. "This looks scrumptious, Sophie."

"I can get my day's worth of fruits and veggies out of the way with just this salad," Charles commented impishly winking at Sarah.

Timothy piled the lasagna high on his plate and passed up the salad bowl altogether. Sophie frowned and passed it back to him. "Yes, Mommy," he responded as Caitlyn and Penny looked at one another and giggled.

Conversation during the meal was light and Penny seemed at ease as long as no one questioned her directly. She and Caitlyn sat across from each other and seemed comfortable. Caitlyn appeared to be considerably older than Penny, but she'd had to grow up fast. After her mother was gone, she had even lived on the street for some months before her real father, Andy, found her. Penny, on the other hand, had lived off-the-grid in Alaska, was home schooled and knew little about the outside world. *It's a strange match*, Sarah thought, *but hopefully they'll find a connection. Caitlyn may not realize it, but they need each other.*

It was decided to have coffee and dessert later and there was general chaos in the kitchen as the women, including Caitlyn and Penny, cleared the table and the men strategized about removing the two extensions from the table. "Would all the men clear out of here please," Sophie announced with exasperation. "We need the bigger table for dessert and coffee."

Once they were gone, Martha said, "How about you girls take Emma for a walk while we get the dishwasher loaded." They both smiled, relieved to be excluded from the cleanup process. "We'll clean up after dessert," Caitlyn offered, looking toward Penny for agreement. Penny nodded and ran to get Emma's leash.

Once they were gone, Sophie reached for the dishtowel and dried her hands. She then reached for Martha and, much to Martha's surprise, enveloped her in a hug. She then stepped back and said, "Thank you for helping to make Penny comfortable. She really relaxed once you brought her in the kitchen and included her in the work. You made her feel like a part of the family."

"Well, that's what she is," Martha said.

"And so are you," Sophie replied, "and I don't just mean if you marry my son. You and your mother and Charles are family to me, and I don't want that to ever change, no matter what happens with you and Tim."

"I appreciate that," Martha responded softly blinking back the tears that were threatening to appear.

Later Tim explained to Martha that he and his mother had been talking about his future and he had shared with her the fact that they had put all talk of marriage aside for the time being.

"So much is up in the air," he had told her. He needed to get Penny settled in school, find a place to live, and hopefully find a job. He felt he was too young to be retired in the usual sense. Tim and his mother had also talked about Martha's reservations about becoming a stepmother at this point in her life.

Chapter 14

Charles arrived at the offices of Kirkland International at exactly ten in the morning. "May I help you?" the young receptionist asked.

"Detective Parker to see Joseph Kirkland."

"Do you have an appointment?" she asked with a frown as she shuffled through the papers on her desk searching for her boss' calendar. Locating it, she responded, "I don't see..."

"No, I don't have an appointment, but I'd like to see Mr. Kirkland this morning. I'm investigating a homicide case and Mr. Kirkland has been identified as a person of interest. Please tell him I'm here."

The young woman appeared flustered, clearly unable to decide on the better course of action. She'd been told emphatically not to disturb her boss, but the man in front of her was adamant about seeing him. After trying unsuccessfully to put the detective off until a later time, she decided to let Kirkland make the decision.

She tapped gently at the door and the angry response was thundering. "Get away from that door!"

"But Mr. Kirkland, I think this might be important..."

"And who gave you permission to think?" he yelled as he swung the door open. "I thought I was perfectly clear..." Looking beyond his receptionist he saw a tall, distinguished man in a navy suit and tie. The man was holding up a shield. Kirkland had no way of knowing how proud the man was to have his shield back, if only temporarily.

"Detective Parker," the man with the shield announced. "I need a few minutes of your time on the Hawkins murder."

"Murder?" Kirkland replied, dismissing the young woman with a hand gesture. "I thought the guy died of old age."

"That's exactly what I'm here to discuss with you."

"With me? I know nothing about it."

"May I have a few minutes of your time?" Charles said in a tone that didn't suggest it was a question. He was still holding his shield in the air.

"Of course," he responded begrudgingly. "Come in. Stephanie, bring coffee."

Charles followed the man into his office and was surprised at the lavish interior. He had been less than impressed when he arrived at the building, which appeared to be an old warehouse. The lobby had been nondescript and the security guard sat behind what appeared to be an old oak salvage desk. Kirkland's office, on the other hand, was pristine. The walls were painted stark white and the outside wall had been replaced by six floor-to-ceiling windows overlooking the park. Two large potted palms appeared like quotation marks on either side of the windows.

One side of the room offered lounge seating with two burgundy leather couches. One massive piece of art hung on the wall – white with random strokes of gray, burgundy, and blue. An open door beyond the lounge area revealed a conference room with a long black table and black leather chairs.

Charles followed Kirkland to his desk that was also black, severe, and totally empty once the man slid the file folder he had been working on into the top drawer. Kirkland motioned for the detective to take a seat across from him. As Kirkland sat, he asked in a modulated tone, "What can I do for you, detective?"

Before Charles could speak, the young woman entered the room carrying a tray with coffee cups and accouterments. She sat the tray on the side bar and added cream and sugar to the cup she offered Kirkland. She then looked at the detective and raised an eyebrow.

95

"Black," he responded. "Thank you."

Once she slipped out of the room and closed the door behind her, Kirkland repeated his question.

"As I said earlier," Charles began, "we're investigating the possible homicide of Earl Hawkins. I'd like to discuss your involvement with the deceased."

"My involvement? I had no involvement. The old guy and I discussed my organization purchasing his property, but he was not interested. I'm currently working with the grandson on that. I only saw the old man a couple of times. There was no involvement, as you put it. What's this all about, detective?"

Ignoring Kirkland's question, Charles continued. "What is your interest in the property, Mr. Kirkland?"

Kirkland appeared to be deciding whether to answer the detective's questions but finally sighed and began talking. He offered a somewhat modified description of the project, downplaying both the size and exclusivity of the development. His tone suggested that the Hawkins property was of little interest to him.

"I understand," Charles continued, "that the Hawkins land was critical to the project since it overlooks the lake."

Kirkland unsuccessfully attempted to hide his agitation. "We can go several ways with that," he finally said.

"And you're working with the grandson now?"

"Yes."

"How long have you known Travis Hawkins?"

"The grandson? I met him at the funeral."

"You attended Earl Hawkins' funeral?" Charles asked incredulously. "That's unusual. You hardly knew the man..."

"Wait a minute," Kirkland yelled, slapping his hand on the desk as he stood. "What's going on here? Am I a suspect? And if so, I want my lawyer here immediately...Stephanie?" he yelled toward the door.

"You don't need a lawyer, Mr. Kirkland," Charles said calmly. "At least not yet..." he added as he stood.

Kirkland's face was flushed with anger. "Get out. My lawyer will contact you and all future discussions will take place through him." Stephanie had just opened the door and looked at the two men questioningly. "Show Mr. Parker out," Kirkland demanded.

* * *

"How was your morning?" Sarah asked. She and Charles had stopped at Sophie's to pick up Emma and were walking both dogs to the park. Emma was holding her head high, complementing the curl of her tail. Barney climbed up and down the snow drifts that were piled high along the road while Emma stepped daintily along the cleared walkway.

"I met with the guy who's planning the resort on the Timberlake Village land. Well, I guess I should say on the Kirkland land. He owns it all except for the Hawkins lot, and it sounds like that's in the works now."

"How's that? Has the estate been settled?"

Charles laughed at the word estate but then realized there was, in fact, a sizeable estate considering Travis Hawkins could probably name his price. "I'll be looking at that next. I assume the grandson is handling all that, at least if he can stay sober long enough to handle the details."

They had arrived at the enclosed dog park and unsnapped both dog's leashes. It was Emma's first visit and she was ecstatic, running excitedly around the entire perimeter and ending up back by Charles. She was panting and appeared to be smiling. Charles took the ball out of his pocket and threw it. Barney, knowing the rules, ran to retrieve it while Emma watched with curiosity. The next time Charles threw the ball, both dogs ran after it and struggled to be the one who would return it. "She catches on fast," Charles commented. "I'll bring two balls next time."

"Do you think Kirkland is involved in Hawkins' death?" Sarah asked.

"He's used to getting his way. He's capable, but I can't say he did it."

"How about the grandson?"

"I need to know more about him. I called the local sheriff's office in Buckner, but they didn't have much on him, just a few speeding tickets and a DUI charge that was dropped. It's hard to get a feel for the guy from that."

"You need to go there?"

"Ideally. I'd like to talk to a few people that know him, but it's an eight-hour drive from here. Would you like to take a road trip with me?"

Sarah thought for a moment. Ruth had asked her to lead the rescue quilt meetings since several members were new quilters and would need instruction. "I don't think so, Charles. Why don't you fly?"

"I looked at that, but at $500 the department would need a better reason for me to be going. Right now, it's just background checking. I might call the sheriff's office again and see if they're willing to send someone out to talk to a few folks for me."

They had been sitting on a bench watching the dogs run and play in the snow. Charles put his arm around his wife and asked if she were cold.

"I'm getting there," she responded.

"Emma, Barney," he called but was completely ignored. He repeated their names, this time one at a time. Each dog came, in turn, and sat by him. "Good dog," he said slipping each a treat as they arrived at his side. Sarah snapped on their leashes, and they headed across the park and through the security kiosk, waving back at their friend Paul as he waved them through.

"Poor Paul," Sarah said once they were out of hearing distance. "Did you hear about his wife?"

"No, what happened?"

"She took the kids and left him. Sophie says he's devastated. He's such a nice guy…"

"One never knows what goes on in other people's lives," Charles responded rather philosophically. "I've often been surprised by what we see when we go into these otherwise respectable-looking homes."

"I know. It's the old two-sides-to-every-story thing, but whatever the reason, the poor guy is suffering and I feel bad for him."

Charles pulled her close to him and kissed her cheek. "You're just an old softy."

"Old?" she repeated, playfully pushing him away. Barney ran to the rescue and planted himself between the two as they continued on their way toward Sophie's house.

Chapter 15

"How did you get connected with this guy in Buckner?" Charles was sitting in Matt Stokely's office discussing the Hawkins case. He had just told his old Lieutenant about the West Virginia investigator who agreed to help on that end.

"I called the Sheriff's office in Buckner again looking for someone to do some legwork for me, and Sheriff Tichner told me about this guy, Bartlett. He's a volunteer with their Deputy Reserves."

"Deputy Reserves?"

"Local folks who volunteer to help out. They get a uniform and usually just supplement the local sheriff's department at events and things like that, but this Bartlett guy, he's older, and he's a retired private detective. They've used him occasionally for simple investigations. Anyway, I offered him a small stipend to help us out. Hope you don't mind…"

Stokely frowned. "How small?"

"A couple hundred for the whole job, including the report."

Stokely sighed. "You needed approval for that, old friend."

"I know. I was on the phone with the guy and decided to take a chance. I'll pay it if the department won't. It's worth it to me to avoid making the trip."

"That trip would cost you as well, and a lot more."

"That's what I figured."

"But I'll approve it. Just submit the bill once you have his report."

"Thanks Matt," Charles said as he stood up and moved toward the door.

"When will he start?" Stokely asked as Charles reached the door.

"He's out there now. I expect to hear from him by the end of the week."

* * *

"Come on in you two," Sophie said hurrying Penny and Caitlyn into the house. The snow had picked up during the short period they had been out with Emma and was approaching blizzard conditions at this point.

"I think I should head on home, Mrs. Ward," Caitlyn responded looking worried.

"Step in here so we can talk about it," Sophie insisted. "I was on the phone with your dad just now and invited the two of you to supper."

"Supper?" Caitlyn repeated looking puzzled.

"Sorry," Sophie responded. "That's an old-time word. When I was growing up we had dinner at noon and the evening meal was called supper. Anyway, your dad said it was fine with him.

"Good," Caitlyn responded, shedding her coat and sitting down on the stool to remove her boots. Penny was busily doing the same but while standing on one foot and tugging on her boot. She looked at Caitlyn and smiled shyly. Penny was beginning to open up with her new family and especially seemed to appreciate Caitlyn's attention. The two girls had become acquainted primarily around the dogs. They often went by and picked up Barney so that they each had a dog to walk, but today they just had Emma.

Emma shook herself hard until all the snow was cleared from her fur and she then laid down on the rug at the front door to lick the snow off her feet. Sophie returned from the kitchen with a damp rag and began wiping her feet. "Why are you doing that?" Penny asked.

"To get the chemicals off that the road crew spread earlier. It helps to melt the snow off the road, but it can really hurt the dog's feet."

Caitlyn smiled as she watched Sophie handling Emma as if she were a small child. One day she had overheard Sarah and her father saying that Emma brought out a side of Sophie that they didn't know she had. "The softer side of Sophie," her father had said.

About that time the door swung open and Timothy came bursting in along with a strong gust of cold air that took them all by surprise. As he was fighting against the wind and attempting to close the door, they heard another voice yell, "Wait for me," and Andy rushed in as well.

"We have five people and a dog all crowded up in this small foyer," Sophie announced. "Let's move all the girls into the living room while you boys get your coats off and knock that snow off your shoes before you come in. Come along, Emma," she added. "You're one of the girls."

Sophie had hot chocolate ready for Caitlyn and Penny, coffee for the adults, and a large dog biscuit spread with peanut butter for Emma. She stood back and watched Penny and Caitlyn interacting with their fathers. Penny was laughing at something Andy had said and she appeared relaxed and happy. As she turned to Sophie, she was still giggling. "Grandmother, did you hear what Caitlyn's dad just said?" Sophie had to fight to hold back the tears that burned the back of her eyes. It was the first time Penny had called her Grandmother.

While her guests warmed themselves, Sophie began scooping chicken and dumplings into individual bowls and placing them on the kitchen table. She pulled a tray of rolls out of the oven and slid them into the bread basket. "Bring your drinks in and sit down," she called happily. Having been alone for many years, it was a joy to have the house full of family and friends. *And a granddaughter*, she marveled. She was still

102

adjusting to the reality of it all. She and Tim had been talking about his plans and it sounded like he would be moving within a month or so, but she intended to enjoy every minute of it until that happened.

Once dinner was served and everyone was eating heartily, Tim spoke up saying, "I got some good news today."

"Oh?"

"I had a call from Mrs. Rankin, the school counselor, today." He looked at Penny with a mischievous smile. "And you, young lady, brought in top scores on your tests."

"I did?" Penny responded cautiously. "What does that mean?"

"That means you'll go right into the high school."

Penny looked apprehensive. "High school?"

"Yes, Mrs. Rankin said you're definitely ready. Your mother did an exceptional job with your home schooling. You scored extremely high in all the eighth grade topics and your math, reading comprehension, and science scores indicated you were right on par with ninth graders."

"But..." Penny sputtered, looking hesitant.

"Don't worry about it, Penny," Caitlyn spoke up. "I finished ninth grade there and I'll help you if you have any problems. They've got really easy teachers anyway. You'll be fine."

Penny looked at the older girl appreciatively. "You think so?"

"I know so. Just stick with me."

The adults chuckled. "You can't go wrong if you stick with this one," Andy said as he tussled his daughter's hair lovingly.

"Dad, stop it," she responded pretending annoyance as she pushed her curls back in place. After a few seconds of silence, she turned to Timothy and asked, "When can she start?"

"Right away. Monday, I guess."

"Great," Caitlyn responded excitedly. "I'll come pick you up and we'll walk together. What are you going to wear?"

"I don't know…"

"Come on. Let's go pick out something for your first day." The two girls slipped out of their chairs and ran to the guest room with Emma right behind them barking with excitement.

Timothy turned to Andy and looked serious. "I don't know how to thank you, man. Your daughter is making it so much easier for Penny. I was worried about her when we first got here…"

"I don't think you have a thing to worry about. I see something in that girl…something I saw in Caitlyn when she first came to live with me. She's a fighter. She's got good genes and her mom's done a great job of building a foundation."

"I didn't want to embarrass her in front of everyone, but her scores were off the chart. Mrs. Rankin said they would be considering her for advanced placement after this term. She scored in the top percentile in both math and science."

"See what I mean?" Andy responded. "Great genes."

"Of course," Sophie interjected proudly. "After all, she's my grandchild."

"Okay Mom. Don't hog all the credit." Sophie smiled lovingly at her son.

Changing the subject, Andy asked about the apartments Timothy was considering. "Well, I've been looking at Collingswood over on Ninth Avenue, but it's a little far from here. I was hoping to be closer to Mom so Penny could go back and forth on her own after I find a job."

"Would you consider a house?"

"I'm not sure I can afford a house until I get a feel for what I'll have coming in."

"I'm asking because there's a little house right up the street. It faces the west end of the park. It's really small, but a friend of mine owns it and he's moving down to Florida to be near his folks."

"He wants to sell it? I don't think…"

"That's just the thing. The realtor told him this is no time to sell. He's looking to rent it. Now, it's small like I said," Andy explained. "It's only got two bedrooms, a small yard in the front and a small area in the back. It might have a basement, but I'm not sure. Oh, there's a garage he uses as a workshop."

"Hmm. Sounds like I should talk to the guy."

Sophie was holding her breath as they talked. The idea of having her son and granddaughter that close was more than she could hope for. Finally she spoke up and added, "You know, if you get a job Penny could come over here after school. She could do her homework here and she'd have Caitlyn right up the street…"

"Tell your friend I'm interested," Timothy said abruptly to Andy. "When can you talk to him?"

"Is now soon enough? I could call him…" The two men hurried into the living room and Andy placed the call. Sophie could tell they were discussing the details and her son sounded excited. They seemed to be talking about meeting the following day if the roads were plowed. She heard her son say, "What do you mean plowed? We can walk over there."

Sophie sat alone at the table, but for the first time in many years she didn't feel at all alone. "Thank you, Lord," she whispered as Emma came into the room and looked up at her with love.

Chapter 16

"Sorry Charlie, there's just not that much to report -- a couple of speeding tickets is all," Bartlett said in an apologetic tone. "Neighbors liked him. He was living with a girl over by the college, and she figured they'd be getting married in a year or two. He'd been with Maxton Office Supply for the past ten years and was taking computer classes to get a promotion..."

"Computer classes?" Charles tried to imagine whiskey-swigging Travis sitting in a classroom and had to smile. "You never know about a guy..."

"Yeah, I feel bad taking your money on this one. The guy was clean. Now I have to admit, he had a couple of unsavory looking friends. I had trouble lining that up in my mind. Don't know why he'd hang out with these guys, but you never know what makes a man pick his friends. I suppose our young Mr. Hawkins could have been experimenting with drugs or something, but I'm telling you for sure, he was clean when he died."

"*Died*? What do you mean died? Who died?"

The detective was stunned for a moment by Charles' reactions. When he spoke he asked, "Are you okay, Charlie? We're talking about your guy Travis Hawkins, aren't we?"

"You've lost me, Bartlett," Charles finally responded. "The guy I'm talking about is very much alive. Travis Hawkins, thirty-five year old grandson of Earl Hawkins?"

"We're talking about the same guy. I'm sorry to have to tell you, Charlie, but Travis Hawkins, son of Earl Hawkins is laying six feet under right here in Buckner, and he's been there since the accident last summer. Everybody here knows that. I just assumed you were looking into his death..."

106

Charles sat down and continued to hold the phone but was speechless. When he finally spoke, he simply said, "I don't know what's going on here, Bartlett, but I'm going to need to keep you on the payroll until we get this straightened out."

The two men talked for another half hour with Charles explaining about the Travis Hawkins imposter he'd been dealing with.

* * *

The cabin was empty when Charles arrived and the car was gone. Charles knocked again just to make sure and then tried the door. It was locked. He walked around to the side and saw there were two windows partially ajar. He thought about slipping through the window, but he was on the department payroll right now and had to follow the rules. He continued on around the cabin and saw that the window into the kitchen stood wide open. *Must be really cold in there*, he told himself.

Charles walked up the three steps to the small porch and tried the door. It was locked. None of the windows were covered, and he could see all the way through to the front. He was still standing there fighting the urge to slip in through the window when he heard a car pull up out front.

As he cleared the corner of the house, he stood face to face with the person he knew as Travis Hawkins. "Afternoon, Travis," Charles said with as friendly a tone as he could manage. "Glad you're home."

"And why is that?" the man pretending to be Travis responded.

"I wanted to talk to you about this Kirkland guy. I understand you've met him...?"

"I've met him. He wants this land really bad."

"Are you considering selling it to him?"

"Might. Just might." The man who wasn't Travis looked nervous as he fidgeted with the zipper on his jacket. "How about a drink?" he finally asked and Charles accepted.

After pouring straight whiskey into two mason jars the man led Charles into the living room and pointed him to the couch as he pushed newspapers aside to make space to set the drinks down. He then went around the house closing the windows and cussing under his breath. "Damn fool woman," Charles heard him say.

"Woman?" Charles said as the man returned to the living room.

"Cleaning lady came by today, said grandpa paid her to clean up. I let her do it and paid her and told her not to come back."

Once the windows were closed, the man tossed a couple of logs on the fire and picked up his drink. He pulled a straight chair up close to the fireplace and took a large gulp of his drink. He closed his eyes and let the liquid warm him up from the inside.

The two men sat quietly as men often do before engaging in conversation. Sophie called it "sizing up the competition." Finally Charles spoke asking the man about his negotiations with Kirkland. He kept his questions casual, not wanting to tip the man off. He realized he must have gone too far when the man suddenly straightened up and said, "Why all the questions? What's your interest in this?"

"I'll have to be honest with you, Travis," Charles began slowly, trying to hide the fact that he was thinking by the seat of his pants. "I might be interested in getting in on this deal of Kirkland's. He's offering some shares and my wife thinks I should take him up on it. You know, this thing of his could really take off..."

The man relaxed. "I don't know. He talks it down with me, but he's trying to get this property as cheap as he can. He's probably trying to con me, but you can't con..." The man didn't finish the sentence and Charles didn't encourage him. He just nodded his head expressing silent understanding. "Another drink?" the man asked.

"Sure."

The man that wasn't Travis sat his glass down and went into the bathroom closing the door behind him. Charles could hear him talking but couldn't make out what he was saying. *He must be on his cell,* Charles thought, wondering who he was calling.

A few minutes later the man, still on the phone, moved into the kitchen. "Okay. I'll bring it in tomorrow," he was saying.

The imposter then ambled back into the living room carrying the bottle and began filling Charles' glass. Charles put his hand up to indicate when to stop. "Just a couple fingers," he said. "The wife's waiting dinner."

The man nodded, walked over to his chair, and looked around on the floor. "Now where the hell did I put that damn jar?" He went back into the bathroom and from there went into the kitchen. "Hell. There's plenty more where that one came from," he muttered as he reached for another mason jar.

The windows were bare and night had fallen. The men sipped their drinks and watched the snow begin to fall. They talked about the weather and about ice fishing on the lake, something Charles was reluctant to try. He'd seen too many men dragged out when they misjudged the thickness of the ice. Finally, Charles stood and thanked the man for the drinks.

"Don't you get lonesome out here alone, Travis?" he asked, again just making friendly conversation.

"Nah. I'm used to it," the man responded walking Charles to the door. "But stop by when you get thirsty," he added lifting his glass to emphasize the offer.

Charles nodded and stepped cautiously across the icy porch and on out to his car, which was now covered with snow. "You need help with that?" the man called out to him.

"I got it, thanks," Charles responded running his coat sleeve over the windshield. He suddenly felt a need to get away from the cabin as quickly as possible. *I'll clean the rest off down the road,* he told himself.

Once he reached the main road he pulled over and pulled on his gloves. He then carefully grasped the mason jar and pulled it out of his pocket. He slipped it into an evidence bag that was waiting on the front seat.

"Mission accomplished," he said to himself aloud with a satisfied smile.

Chapter 17

"Timmy and I are on our way to look at the house and see what they'll need. Do you want to go with us?"

"I'd love to, Sophie," Sarah responded "Can you give me a few minutes to finish up here?"

"About 10:30 then?"

"Perfect," Sarah replied. "I'll meet you outside," she added and hung up.

Timothy and Penny had looked at the rental house by the park and loved it. It turned out to be bigger than Andy had described with a third bedroom that they decided to turn into a study for the two of them. The owner preferred to rent the house furnished, and Tim said this worked well for him since he wasn't sure about his long-range plans. Sarah and Sophie had looked at one another when he said that, wondering what that meant as far as Timothy and Martha were concerned.

Once they arrived at the house, Timothy led Sarah around and explained what he had in mind. As there was already a desk in the third bedroom, Timothy said this would be their study. He was going to buy Penny a computer of her own, and he would continue to use his laptop and iPad. Sophie offered to give them her futon for that room in case they ever needed extra sleeping space.

The rooms were relatively small, with a master bedroom that contained a full-sized bed and a dresser. There was a slightly larger room that Timothy said would be Penny's room, "since girls need space for primping." There were two twin beds in Penny's room that Sophie thought would be good if she wanted to have sleepovers once she made some friends.

The living room was adequately furnished, but the sofa and chairs were rather worn. "There's storage space in the garage," Timothy said, "and the owner told me I could store any of his furniture we don't need. I might buy a new couch and a couple of chairs for the living room. We'll need it eventually anyway."

"How did Penny like the house," Sarah asked as she followed Timothy toward the kitchen.

"She loved it. This house is more than twice as big as the cabin she and her mother had in Alaska. And," he added, "they were still using the outhouse until a couple of years ago."

"This must look like a mansion to her," Sophie speculated.

"She was really happy about having her own room. I'm taking her to the mall after school so she can pick out her bedding and a curtain for the window."

"She also needs new clothes," Sophie added, but Tim responded with a puzzled look. "I guess we could look..."

"We'll take her this weekend," Sophie offered looking at Sarah with a questioning look."

Sarah nodded her agreement and smiled. "It'll be fun having a girl to shop for again."

Sophie led the group into the kitchen. The appliances were old but certainly adequate for a bachelor and his daughter. *Sophie will probably be sending food over for them*, Sarah thought. She then opened the refrigerator and found it stocked with fresh food. She laughed when she opened the freezer door and found it already filled with casserole dishes.

"So I couldn't let them starve, could I?" Sophie responded defensively.

"Do you want to see the basement?" Timothy offered. "Actually, there's nothing to see down there. It's partially finished and the washer and dryer are down there. It looks like the guy was planning to finish it himself but he didn't get very far."

"I'll pass," Sarah said knowing that it would be difficult for Sophie to negotiate the narrow stairway.

112

"Me too," Sophie chimed in.

"How about the garage?"

"I'll leave that for Charles. I think he'll enjoy seeing it. Sophie said it's full of old tools and a couple of unfinished projects. Where did this guy go anyway?"

"He went down to Florida to take care of his parents. His father needs to be in a nursing home but refuses to go, and his mother isn't able to take care of him. John said he'll probably sell the house and stay down there, but he wants to try it out first."

As they were getting back into the Pup Mobile, Tim laid his hand on Sarah's arm. "I'm glad you gals are taking Penny out shopping. Maybe you can get her to talk."

"What do you mean?"

"For several nights now I've heard her crying after she went to bed. One night I tapped on the door, but when I opened it she pretended to be asleep. I tried to talk to her about it, but she just looks embarrassed and says it's nothing."

"She's missing her mother, Tim," Sarah replied.

"But I'm trying to give her the best life I can," he responded with a worried frown. "I don't know..."

"Tim, you can't make her pain go away. She has to mourn and if she wants to do that alone, just let her be."

"I hate to think of her in there alone and hurting..."

"I know, and you want to fix it. But some things can't be fixed and actually, some things shouldn't be fixed. She needs to feel her feelings and work through them. What you need to watch for is any signs that she's not working them through."

"What do you mean?"

"Some people, especially young people, end up acting out. You need to be on the alert for any of those signs – excessive anger, defiance, depression, even possible drug use."

Timothy suddenly looked panicked. "What have I gotten myself into? I don't know how to raise a daughter and what if..."

"Timothy, you are perfectly capable of this and you're the best person for the job. You're her father. But remember, you have lots of folks to help you. We're all here for you and for Penny." She reached over and pulled him into a comforting hug. "I didn't mean to scare you. I guess what it all boils down to is that Penny is exactly where she should be right now. She's in a loving home and she's dealing with her grief. Just be there for her, listen if she wants to talk, and remember that we're all behind you." She saw a tear forming in his eyes, yet he was smiling.

"Thank you, Aunt Sarah," he responded lovingly.

"Aunt Sarah it is now, huh?" she responded with a chuckle. "I guess we're a lot like family, aren't we?" ...*and we just might really be family one of these days,* she thought but didn't say.

As they pulled away from the curb, Sophie blew her new barking horn.

* * *

"What are you doing here?" Kirkland demanded angrily as Charles stepped into the office.

Kirkland's receptionist burst in right behind him apologetically saying, "I'm sorry, sir. I couldn't stop him..."

Ignoring his receptionist, Kirkland again demanded, "I asked you a question officer. What are you doing in my office?"

"I want to share some information with you, something I think you need to know about the man you're negotiating with."

"There's nothing I need to know. Young Hawkins settled for a tidy amount and is gone." Kirkland picked up a stack of papers that were on his desk and waved them in the air. "And the Hawkins property is mine now, free and clear."

"Possibly not so free and definitely not so clear, Mr. Kirkland. I think you should listen to what I have to say."

114

"I'll give you thirty seconds and no more," the man said dramatically looking at his watch.

Charles reached into this pocket and pulled out a folded newspaper clipping and laid it on Kirkland's desk. He then sat down, knowing he'd be there much longer than thirty seconds. He watched as Kirkland glanced at the article Charles had copied from the Buckner Daily newspaper that described Travis Hawkins' death.

"What's this trash?" Kirkland asked. Without waiting for an answer, he began to read. Charles watched as the arrogance drained from the man's face and was replaced first by a look of dismay and then fear. "What?" he muttered then looked up with an anger that could kill. "What's the meaning of this? He can't be dead. He was in this office just yesterday. He signed these papers," again picking up the papers and shaking them in the air, "and I gave him...oh god, I gave the man half a million dollars in cash..." He put his elbows on the desk and buried his face in his hands. "How could I have been so stupid...?"

Looking up abruptly at Charles, he demanded, "So who signed this? And who did I give the money to?"

"You gave him cash?" Charles responded incredulously. "Why cash?"

The man again buried his face in his hands and shook his head back and forth. "He said he'd sign the papers and go away..." he muttered. "I let my impatience get the better of me...what with the contactors waiting...and the county hounding me..." He didn't finish the sentence. He just sat and muttered, "How could I have been so stupid," not expecting an answer and seeming to be no longer aware of Charles' presence.

"I might be able to help you find him," Charles spoke up saying. "I've asked the medical examiner's office to check a glass for finger prints and possibly even DNA. If she can identify the man..."

"I'll have him strung up!" Kirkland yelled, angrily finishing Charles' sentence.

"I'll let you know what I find out," Charles said as he stood. The man was clearly too overwrought to discuss the matter now. He slipped a card out of his breast pocket and laid it on Kirkland's desk. "Call me when you're ready to talk," he said and walked quickly out the door and past the receptionist.

Chapter 18

"We need to close the shades, turn off all these electronic gadgets we have around here, light a few candles, and sit down in the living room with a glass of wine so we can talk about everything that's going on in our lives. I feel out of touch with the woman I love."

"That sounds like a perfect idea," Sarah responded. "Are you hungry?"

"A little, but I'm not in the mood for dinner yet. I'll open the wine and maybe you could grab us some cheese and crackers."

"Perhaps we'll order pizza later," she suggested as she went into the kitchen to prepare a snack platter. In addition to the cheese and crackers, she opened a container of hummus, sliced an apple, and rinsed off a dozen strawberries. Charles had the wine poured when she returned to the living room and the lights dimmed. There were two candles flickering on the coffee table.

"This is more like it," he said as he put his arm around her. "Now, tell me what you've been up to the past few days. It feels like we've just passed one another like two ships in the night."

Sarah laughed and replied, "It hasn't been quite that bad, dear, but let's see now..." She took a sip of her wine and continued, "...Sophie and I went with Tim to see the new house." Sarah told him all about the house and what she knew about the man who rented it to them. She also told him what Tim had told her about his concerns with Penny. "She's very sad," Sarah added, "and spends a great deal of time closed off in her bedroom."

"She may be sad some of the time," Charles replied, "but she's also enjoying being with Sophie and Tim. You can tell that right away when you spend a little time with them."

"I wonder if she might be feeling a little guilty about enjoying her new life without her mother," Sarah speculated softly. "I think I might feel that way under similar circumstances. I know when I first started falling in love with you, I sometimes felt like I was being disloyal to Jonathan."

"Moving on was hard for both of us. Are you ever sorry?" he asked, already knowing the answer, but he loved hearing it.

She gently punched his arm saying, "You know better than to ask that, you silly man. I've not been sorry for one moment." She reached for the snack platter and made two sandwiches with the cheese and crackers, placing a strawberry on the top of the one she passed to Charles. He removed the strawberry and popped it into her mouth and they both smiled.

"And how about Sophie? Is she adjusting to life as a grandmother?"

"She loves it. When we took Penny shopping for school clothes, Sophie wanted to buy everything in the store. I had to slow her down by telling her if she doesn't buy it all at once, she and Penny can enjoy many more shopping trips. She was even looking at prom dresses!"

"Prom dresses? When is Penny going to a prom?" Charles asked looking puzzled.

"In three or four years!" Sarah responded rolling her eyes. "Penny and I managed to talk Sophie out of it."

They sat quietly for a few minutes while Charles refilled his wine glass and offered Sarah more. "I'm fine," she responded and then added, "Okay, I've told you a bit about my life, but I think you have much more exciting things to tell me. What's happening with the Hawkins case? Last I heard you had learned the man we met at the cabin was an imposter, and you had just taken a glass with fingerprints to the Medical Examiner's office. Any word on that?" Sarah asked.

"Not yet, but I'll be checking in with her in a few days. In the meantime, it seems that the very successful real estate tycoon, Joseph Kirkland, may not be as smart as he thought he was. Last week he handed our impostor an enormous amount of cash in exchange for fraudulent papers claiming to transfer the title of the Hawkins property to him."

"Oh my," she gasped. "Does he know?"

"I told him. Actually, I took him the article from the Buckner newspaper that reported the death of the *real* Travis Hawkins and he was pretty near speechless, at least when he wasn't spouting profanities."

"Will Kirkland report it to the police?"

"I doubt it. I think Kirkland is pretty embarrassed about being conned like that. He's probably going to try to handle it himself. I told him I was looking for the guy for my own reasons and would let him know what I find out."

"Are you going out to the cabin?" she asked, looking worried.

"Kirkland told me that Travis, the fake one that is, was on his way out of town the day he got the money. I haven't confirmed that yet, but it's most likely true. He'd be a fool to hang around after that transaction."

"Shall we drive out tomorrow and see if he's gone?" she asked.

"Hmm. I'm not sure I want to take you out there. If he's still around, it could be dangerous."

"Well, since I would be just as worried about you going, I think it has to be both of us or neither of us..."

"I'll call Matt and ask if he'll send a patrolman out to check the house."

"Good compromise. So, what next?"

Charles contemplated for a few moments and then responded thoughtfully. "I think, first of all, I'll have Bartlett, the Buckner detective, check out those two guys he described as "unsavory friends" of the real Travis. I'd like to know if they've been out of town. One of those guys would be on the top of my list of suspects."

Sarah looked puzzled. "What makes you think they might be involved?"

"Well, they would have known Travis and his story. Remember, when we talked to the fake Travis, he seemed to know lots of details about the Hawkins family and about the cabin. He had enough information to look real. He fooled us," he added. "Those guys were close to the real Travis and would have known what was going on."

"Good point," she responded. "And if they haven't been out of town?"

"I think, either way, I need to get into that cabin and see if there's any evidence that will help me identify this guy in case Charlotte doesn't come up with a name."

"Charlotte?" Sarah repeated, tilting her head and raising an eyebrow.

"You know Charlotte. The medical examiner."

"Oh?" she responded with both eyes brows now raised. "You must mean Dr. Johansson."

"Yes, I mean Dr. Johansson and don't pretend to be jealous, because I know better. You know you have me in your back pocket."

Sarah laughed. "I was just teasing. So, after you have Matt check to make sure that the guy is gone, shall we go take a look inside that cabin? We just might find something...Oh wait!" she added interrupting herself. "The cabin belongs to Kirkland now, doesn't it? We'd need his permission..."

"No," Charles responded. "Remember, the documents were fraudulent. The cabin is still part of the Hawkins estate and there doesn't seem to be anyone around to claim it."

"Will you need a search warrant?"

"I don't see how I could get one. Actually, I'm only loosely connected with the department. I might just take my chances. If we find anything critical to the senior Hawkins case, we'll back out and have Matt get a search warrant. But I'm not looking for evidence of that crime. I'm just hoping to find something that'll put me on the trail of the imposter."

"Are you thinking he killed the old man?" Sarah asked looking serious.

"I have no reason to think one way or the other about that, but I do know the guy is guilty of fraud...and yes, he might have even killed Hawkins."

"When shall we go?" Sarah asked, getting excited about the idea. She enjoyed being included in his sleuthing.

"Once we have assurance the guy's gone, we'll head out there."

"There's something I've been thinking about, Charles. The day we went out there looking for Emma..."

"The day we met Travis...I mean the guy we thought was Travis..." Charles interjected.

"Yes. Well, I've been thinking about how Emma cowered when he came outside. It was as if she knew him and was afraid of him."

"You know, I hadn't really thought about that, but I remember seeing her slink away. That's the reason I had Sophie get in the car and sent the dog in after her. I thought Emma was just upset about being at the house, but you may be right. She may have been responding to seeing the man. Maybe..." He thought back to the night they found the body. He wondered if Emma knew something she couldn't tell.

"Maybe what?" Sarah asked.

"Maybe I need to think more about that. Let's call for that pizza."

He was still feeling uncomfortable about their earlier exchange. "What is it?" she asked, sensing his discomfort.

"About Charlotte, I mean Dr. Johansson..."

Sarah burst out laughing. "Charles, I was just teasing you. Surely you know that?"

"I guess I do. I just wanted to tell you how much I love you."

"I know that, you silly goose," she responded as she kissed his cheek and headed for the phone. "...pizza with everything?" she asked.

"Except anchovies," he responded.

* * *

"Just leave your scraps on the table and we'll sort them when everyone gets here." Ruth had set up a six-foot folding table along the back wall so they could save the workstations for the machines.

"I brought my two yards of dog material. Shall we put the dogs in a separate place?" Delores asked.

"Let's put all the dogs on that end and the skies and grass at this end. That leaves plenty of room in the middle for the scraps. In fact, let me put a basket in the middle." Ruth slipped into the back room and returned with a very large, low-sided basket that she placed in the middle. Everyone began tossing their scraps into the basket. By the time everyone had arrived, the basket was overflowing.

"I suggest we decide on our color scheme," Sarah suggested once everyone was seated. After much discussion, it was decided to use bright primary colors for the dog houses.

"I think we need more variety than just the red, blue, and yellow," Ruth said. "How about including the secondary color as well? I think adding oranges, purples, and greens would make it more interesting."

"I agree," Kimberly responded, "and I think we should weed the other scraps out of the basket so we can see what we have. Does everyone want their own scraps back?"

"Why don't we just start a scrap collection here? We can use it for charity quilts in the future."

"Good idea," Ruth said. "I'll get a box and we can keep it in the store room, but someone needs to be in charge of remembering it's there. My memory is shot!"

"Mine, too."

"Same here. We need a young person. Where's Caitlyn," Christina asked looking toward the door.

"She's not able to come tonight," Sarah responded. "School work took precedence."

"Okay, where do we start?" someone asked.

"Ruth made templates for everyone. We can start by picking out a dog that fits nicely within the template and cut it out. I drew around my template and cut it with scissors, but you can do it any way you want. Then you just start adding strips all the way around until you're happy with it."

"How do you put the sky on?"

"I'll demonstrate that when we get to that point."

Sophie offered to cut strips and pulled a chair up to the stash basket. Sarah brought her a cutting mat and rotary cutter and showed her how to cut strips one-and-a-half inches wide in a variety of colors.

Everyone worked industriously for the next hour and finally two people were ready to add the skies. Sarah showed them how she did it using two pieces of sky fabric. She said there was no need to measure it exactly because they could simply use their ruler to square it up when they finished. "You can add a rectangle of grass or rocks to the bottom of the block." Everyone had stopped working to watch how she did the sky and by nine o'clock everyone had made at least one.

"We have seven finished blocks," Sarah announced as the group was gathering up their supplies. "It's going to take several more meetings to make them all."

"Oh, that reminds me," Ruth interrupted. "I'm having some work done in the shop next week and we'll need to cancel our meeting. Our next meeting will be in two weeks. What would you think about making a few blocks at home?"

"Excellent idea," Delores responded. "Let's quickly cut out some dogs to take with us. We all have fabric at home."

"Grab what you think you might need from the scrap basket."

It was after ten when Ruth was finally able to lock the door behind the last of the excited quilters.

Chapter 19

"Caitlyn, what a surprise," Sarah exclaimed as she opened the front door. "Come on in." The wind was howling, and the temperature had dropped fifteen degrees in the past hour. "You must be freezing, young lady," she said as she helped Caitlyn off with her coat. "There's a major snow storm rolling in," she added. "I don't think this is a good time for you and Barney to be walking."

"Actually," Caitlyn began somewhat hesitantly. "I wanted to talk to you about Penny."

"Penny? Is anything wrong?"

"I'm not sure, Mrs. Parker…"

"What is it Caitlyn?" Sarah was becoming concerned. The young girl seemed reluctant to talk about it and she feared Penny was in some sort of trouble. "Just sit down here and start from the beginning," Sarah encouraged.

"I guess you know that Penny spends most of the time in her room with the door closed."

"Yes, Sophie told me. We figured she needed to be alone to think things through. She's been through so much over the past few months…"

"That's just it, Mrs. Parker…"

"Please call me Sarah, honey. Everyone else does."

"Okay, anyway, Penny needs someone to talk to and she doesn't want to upset her father or her grandmother."

"She talks to you, doesn't she?"

"Yes, she does, and I'm afraid I'm in over my head."

"What do you mean?"

"She keeps telling me she wants to go home. She's trying to figure out how to buy a bus ticket. She doesn't seem to understand that what she remembers as home doesn't exist anymore."

"She must realize that," Sarah responded. "She knows her mother is gone and that the cabin has been sold."

"She knows that, but she still seems to think she can go back and everything will be okay. I don't know what else to say, and I'm afraid she's going to run off and try to get back there. She needs to be talking to an adult about this, but she won't. She just keeps saying, 'I want to go home.' I don't know what to say to her, Sarah, and I was wondering if you could help."

"She should be talking to her father or Sophie."

"I know, and I've told her that. She doesn't want to cause trouble."

"I can assure you that if she runs away she will be causing them more trouble than she can imagine. That would be devastating for them – for all of us, in fact. She's only fourteen and would be placing herself in danger out there alone."

"I know," Caitlyn muttered, lowering her head. "I know."

"I'm sorry, Caitlyn. I don't know what I was thinking. Of course you know." She pulled the young girl close and wrapped her arms around her. Caitlyn had spent months struggling alone on the streets after her stepfather threw her out. "You also know what she's going through now, don't you?" Once Caitlyn was found, she went to live with a father she had never met, in a community of strangers.

Caitlyn nodded her head. "Maybe that's why I don't know what to say. I remember what it was like. I felt like I was in the way too."

"Penny feels like she's in the way?" Sarah responded with astonishment. "No one was ever as loved as that young girl is. I've never seen Sophie or Tim so happy – she's brought so much joy to their lives."

126

"I guess she doesn't see that."

"Is she unhappy with her new family?"

"No, that's not it at all. She's homesick, she misses her mother, and I think she just wants everything back the way it was. What she wants doesn't exist anymore and I'm afraid she's going to try to find it anyway. I don't know how to help her..." Tears began to form in the young girl's eyes. "Can you help?"

"Of course I'll try, but what do you think I can do?"

"She needs to talk. She's holding onto so many painful memories and feelings. She needs for someone to help her find the words. It took me several years before I'd talk about my experiences on the streets, and I almost made some very bad decisions during that time. Fortunately my dad encouraged me to talk. He'd been through a lot himself, and he could listen without judging me. She just needs help to find the words to express what's going on inside."

Sarah remained quiet for a few moments. "Do you think she'd consider counseling?"

"I don't think so. Can't you talk to her?" Caitlyn pleaded. "You know her and she likes you. She might open up with you..."

"Oh Caitlyn, I just don't know. I'd feel like I was interfering in a family matter. It should be Tim or Sophie."

"But she won't talk to them. I know that."

Sarah sighed deeply. "I need to think about this, Caitlyn."

"Okay," Caitlyn responded looking somewhat relieved.

"Now, let's take Barney in the kitchen and get treats for all three of us. Do you want a coke or hot chocolate?"

"I'm still cold and hot chocolate sounds great."

"Good. Will you choose a few treats for Barney?" They spent the next half-hour on a lighter note. After their snacks, Sarah showed Caitlyn the dog house quilt blocks she was working on. Caitlyn's school work had made it impossible for

127

her to attend the workshop, but she was hoping to make at least one block before the next meeting.

"I wonder if Penny knows about this quilt," Caitlyn asked.

"Probably," Sarah said thoughtfully. "I'm sure Sophie has told her about it." She hesitated for a moment and then said, "This gives me an idea."

"What?"

"I'm planning to make Penny a quilt for her new bedroom. Maybe I could invite her to help me choose the fabrics. Actually," she added with growing enthusiasm, "maybe she could even help me make it."

"That would give you two time together -- time to talk. She just might open up," Caitlyn added with growing enthusiasm.

"Exactly what I was thinking."

Together they put the blocks and fabric back in the pizza box. "I have a week to finish these. I think I'll give her a call today and see if she wants to go with me to Stitches."

As they walked toward the front door, Barney became excited at the possibility of going for a walk. "Sorry boy," Caitlyn said tenderly. "It's much too cold out there today." She turned to Sarah and said, "Thank you, Sarah. I was really scared. I didn't know what to say to her, and I was afraid I'd do the wrong thing."

"That was too much responsibility for you. I'm glad you came to me. I'll let you know how it goes, but I've got to tell you that if I can't reach her, I'll have to talk with Tim and Sophie."

"I know. I didn't want to do that myself. I think she needs my friendship and, for that matter, I need hers. I'm afraid we'd lose that if I went to her family."

"I agree. You did the right thing." They hugged their goodbyes and Sarah headed straight for the telephone.

"Hi Sophie. Are you keeping warm?"

"It's cozy in the house, and I have no intentions of going out. What's up?"

128

"I've been thinking about the quilt I want to make for Penny. I can't decide what colors to use. I was hoping she'd go with me to Stitches after school today and help me..."

"She's right here. School was cancelled today because of the storm. Are you sure you want to go out in it?"

"It's just windy and cold. They don't expect the snow until later."

"Penny," Sophie called. "Telephone for you."

"Hello?" the young voice answered tentatively.

"Penny, it's Sarah." She went on to tell her about the quilt and asked if she'd be willing to go with her to choose the fabrics. "I was even hoping you might help me make it. I know Caitlyn quilts and I thought you might like to learn as well."

There was an extended silence on the other end of the line.

"Penny?" Sarah suspected the confused young girl was thinking how this would interfere with her desire to return to Alaska. Sarah hoped what she was offering would entice Penny to set those thoughts aside at least for the time being.

"I think I'd like to do that," she said finally, "but I don't know anything about fabric."

"You know what you like — what designs and what colors appeal to you. We'll just walk through the aisles until something reaches out and grabs you."

Sarah thought she heard a faint giggle on the other end of the line. "Okay," Penny responded. "Are you going today?"

"Yes, I think we can make it before the snowfall."

"When are you leaving?"

"How about right now?"

* * *

The snow had come the previous night as predicted and the school board anticipated schools being closed for the rest of the week. There was eighteen inches of snow already, and it was still coming down. Charles had fired up the propane fireplace and Tim had followed the snow plow up the road in order to deliver Penny. "You just might get snowed in here," he told her as he was leaving. Sarah had assured him that would be fine with them. "We'll sew all night," she had said playfully.

"I love this fabric," Penny was saying as she pressed out the creases before cutting the strips. "Are you sure I should cut it? I'm afraid I'll ruin it."

"I'll show you how and cut a few strips first, but remember, there's plenty more where this came from," she added casually. She wanted to show Penny that quilting could be fun and relaxing. She could tell the girl had a tendency to take things very seriously, and she was afraid she'd have trouble learning to enjoy quilting.

They had found a simple star pattern in a beginning quilting book that they both liked and Penny had spotted a playful piece of fabric with stylized cats in bright shades of hot pink, purple, blue, and green. The cats were crowded close together and were outlined in gold with a curly tail and gold whiskers. Fearing that Penny would soon tire of such a bold pattern, Sarah suggested tone-on-tones to go with it to help soften the overall look. They decided to place the cats in the center of the star with the points made of the simpler fabrics. They chose an off-white background and planned to use strips of the cat fabric for the borders.

"How long will it take to make this?" Penny asked.

"I think we can finish it this week. It's really an easy pattern. Once you get a few strips cut, I'll start sewing." Sarah had already cut the borders and the star centers. "Of course, it'll still need to be quilted. I'll take it to Judy as soon as we finish."

"Judy?"

"Judy does the quilting for me. She has a long-arm quilting machine." Penny looked confused. Sarah pulled out one of her quilts and went over the part of the quilt: the top, the batting, and the back. She explained how the three layers were patiently and methodically sewn together in the old days by hand but went on to tell her about Judy's long-arm quilting machine. "I'll take you to her house to see it if you'd like."

"That would be fun. I'd love to see it," Penny responded enthusiastically. "Maybe we can go after school next week." *She's beginning to make plans for the future*, Sarah told herself. *That's a very good sign!* But she knew they had a long way to go. Caitlyn had been right when she said Penny needed to talk about her feelings. She was keeping too much pain inside.

Sarah promised herself she would be patient.

Chapter 20

"Sophie, calm down. What's happened? Is it Penny?"

"Yes, it's Penny," Sophie said breathlessly, "and I have no idea what to do. Can you come over and help me?"

"Sophie, I'll help you, but you've got to tell me what's going on." Reflecting on things she had learned from Caitlyn, Sarah feared the worst. *I hope she hasn't announced her unrealistic plan to go to Alaska.*

"It's a boy."

"*What's* a boy?" Sarah asked, now confused.

"She brought a boy home from school with her."

"And?"

"Don't you get it? She has a boy here." Sophie had been whispering, but her voice was beginning to rise.

"What are they doing, Sophie?"

"They're doing homework in the kitchen, but..."

"But what?"

"But I don't know if he should be here. Penny's only fourteen, and..."

"Sophie, I think this is fine. I'll come over if you really need me, but I don't think this is anything to worry about. I'm actually glad to hear she's making friends. He's her age, right."

"Yes," Sophie said sighing.

"Why don't you go fix them a snack, and maybe you could find something to do in the kitchen so you can see that everything is fine." At that moment, Sarah heard laughing in the background. "Was that the kids?"

"Yes."

"Sophie, if this boy can make her laugh, I think we should all be thankful that she found him. That sad young girl needs a good laugh. In fact, with your outrageous sense of humor, I think you should work on making her laugh as well."

"I'm sort of tied in knots around her. I don't know kids, you know?" There was a pause and Sophie said, "Someone's at the door. Hold on a second." Sarah heard Sophie opening the door and could hear her welcoming someone to the house. She returned to the phone a different person.

"It's Andy and Caitlyn. They're on their way to the park and stopped by to pick up Emma and Penny. I'll send the boy along with them. Andy can tell me what he thinks when they get back. Thanks anyway, Sarah. I think everything is going to be okay." She hung up leaving Sarah holding the phone and shaking her head.

"It's going to take our Sophie some time to get used to having a teenager in the house," she said to Charles who had just come in from the garage.

Sarah sat down with a cup of coffee and thought about all the changes in Sophie's life. "You look far away," Charles commented as he poured himself a cup.

"I was thinking about Sophie and all her new ventures – the Pup Mobile, becoming a grandmother, and now helping out at the quilt club. It's pretty amazing."

"I think her whirlwind romance with Higginbottom last year was a turning point for her," Charles speculated.

"You're probably right. That experience motivated her to get her knee replacement and she's been much more active since then. And if you notice," Sarah added, "she went into grandmothering, and even quilting, with excitement instead of her usual reluctance."

"Don't discount the part you've played in all this," Charles added.

"No. I haven't done anything. She's done this all herself."

"Okay, she's done it, but you've been a very positive influence on her and a very good friend to her. You're the one who got her onto that cruise ship a couple of years ago, and you brought our Barney into her life, helping her to learn what she was missing by not having a pet to love."

"I suppose I sort of nagged her into the knee replacement..." Sarah added reluctantly.

"And she's been out there detecting with you despite the police department threatening you both with jail time if you didn't stay out of their cases..."

Sarah laughed. "I guess my influence hasn't always been the best..."

* * *

"Do you have anything for me?" Charles asked as he entered the Medical Examiner's office. Dr. Charlotte Johansson raised her head from the microscope and smiled. She wished she could return to the old days when Charlie Parker was on the force. *Things were better then*, she told herself. *More human*.

"Charlie, am I ever glad to see you. It's been a madhouse around here today. Do you have time for a cup of coffee? I just brewed a pot."

Charles accepted the offer and sat down in the small kitchenette with Charlotte. They had been good friends back in the day and he, too, was glad to see her. He was always able to count on her to bring sensitivity and logic to his cases.

Years ago he would sit in this little make-shift kitchen sipping coffee and going over evidence with his friend. He had even wondered back then if there could possibly be a future for the two of them, but it quickly became evident that they were destined only for friendship.

Charlotte set a cream-filled pastry in front of him along with a mug of coffee already prepared with double cream and sugar, the way he always drank it in the old days. Not wanting to hurt her feelings, he accepted it with a smile and didn't point out that he could no longer enjoy these little extravagances. He knew Sarah would not be pleased but also knew she would understand why he made the exception. At least, these are the things he told himself as he rationalized the extravagance.

"So tell me," he began after a period of polite conversation and a few heavenly bites of the pastry. "What have you learned?"

"Okay. Here it is. I was able to pick up a few good prints and if you find the guy, I'll be able to match the prints for you. But the prints aren't in the system. I can't tell you who he is," she said regretfully.

Charles lowered his head and shook it. He was disappointed, knowing that it was unlikely they would ever find the man now. He took another sip of his coffee but without his original enthusiasm.

"But it's not all bad news," Charlotte added.

Charles lifted his head and looked at his friend hopefully. "Tell me."

"I was able to get several DNA samples from saliva around the rim of the glass." Charles remembered lifting the glass from his pocket by the rim and was thankful he hadn't damaged the sample.

"And?" he asked.

"And I sent it off to the lab. It'll take a couple of weeks, Charlie. I'm sorry, but at least there's hope."

"Well, that's true but DNA doesn't give me a name if he's not in the system."

"True, but it gives you something you don't have now. I'll call you the second we get something from them. I marked it as a priority, but if anything comes in through the official channels..."

"I know, I know. My request gets bumped."

"It's not like the old days…," she said, "when the lab would give top priority to anything coming to them from the illustrious Detective Charles Parker."

"Nope," he responded, knowing exactly what she meant. For Charles, retirement didn't just mean giving up his job. It meant giving up the place he'd gone every day for thirty years, having a routine, a purpose, a career, office friends, and co-workers. But of all the losses Charles had to face with his retirement, he felt the most impact from the loss of his status within the police department. He had served for many years and, as a lead detective, he was respected by his superiors and looked up to by the younger officers. He told himself he was being vain, but the fact was – he missed it all.

"I'll be in touch," Charlotte said walking back toward her lab and abruptly shaking him out of his reverie.

As he was leaving the room, he handed her his business card with his cell and home numbers. "Thanks Charlotte."

Chapter 21

"Why are we going to the airport?" Penny asked timidly as the small private airport came into view.

"This is where we're picking up the dogs."

"They're coming on an airplane?" she asked looking surprised.

"This time they are," Sophie responded with a broad smile. Sophie was proud to be part of the rescue network and, once she parked the van in front of the office of the small private airport, she turned to her granddaughter and explained that there were people who owned small planes who volunteered to carry rescued dogs and cats from city to city. "That way the animals don't have to spend so much time on the road. This man, I think his name is Roy, is carrying three dogs to Chicago and he agreed to stop here with these two little Pekingese."

"Where is he coming from?"

"Somewhere in Kansas, I think. Maybe Wichita," Sophie responded. "Let's take a look at the paperwork. Sophie reached into the side pocket and pulled out several computer pages clipped together and entitled Final Run-Sheet. "Okay, here it is. They're names are Molly and Polly and they're two-year old females."

"What's that you're reading from?"

"It's the run-sheet. Everyone along the way gets a copy and that way we all know who we're transporting, where to pick them up, and where to take them. Look here," she said pointing to the second page. "See, we are picking them up at Middletown Regional Airport and taking them to this address."

Penny looked at the address. "Is this a no-kill shelter like you were telling me about?"

"No," Sophie said with a wide smile. "That's the address of their forever home. These little girls are sisters and they're very lucky. They've been adopted together."

About that time they heard a roar and looked up to see a small plane circling the field.

"I'll bet this is Roy," Sophie announced and the two hurriedly got out of the van and headed for the office. Once inside, Sophie approached a man sitting at a desk behind a sign that read, "Fixed Base Operator." She explained why they were there and introduced Penny who was, of course, embarrassed by the attention. *Will I ever remember what it was like to be fourteen?* she chastised herself.

"That's your guy coming in right now," the FBO responded, "in that single-engine Cessna out there. Once he's turned his engines off, you can walk on out and meet him." Sophie was surprised to see how animated Penny became once they were out on the tarmac. She ran ahead of her grandmother and arrived at the plane just as the pilot was opening the door.

"Do you have our dogs?" she asked the man, again surprising Sophie with her lack of shyness. "May I see them?" she asked before the pilot had a chance to answer her first question.

"You bet I have them. Would you like to step into the plane so you can see them?"

"May I?" she asked, now looking a bit reticent.

"You sure may." Looking toward Sophie, he asked, "Is it okay?"

"Sure," Sophie responded. "I wish I could get my stiff bones up there, but I'll wait out here. Go on in, Penny," she encouraged and Penny hopped onto the plane.

Once inside, the young girl was taken aback by the four kennels lined up in the make-shift cargo section. Two were large and each contained a big dog. "Is that a Collie?" she asked pointing to the long-haired dog with gentle eyes.

138

"Yes," Roy responded. "That's Angie and this is Bear over here. He's a Golden Retriever mix, I think." There was a small travel crate with a tiny white Chihuahua laying on a blanket looking up at her with terror in his eyes as if he were pleading for her help.

"Aww," she said, looking back at him sadly. "Oh look," Penny squealed suddenly as she looked into the fourth kennel. Inside were two small brown furry dogs with flat wrinkled faces, big round eyes, and wagging tails. "They're so cute," she said as she got down on her knees in front of the kennel. "Are these ours?"

"Those are your girls," Roy responded, reaching back to lift the kennel forward. "I was lucky I had room for them. I just had three seats removed to make more cargo space."

The two little Pekingese puppies wiggled with excitement as they tried to get to Penny. "Look at their little flat faces," Penny squealed. "They're so cute." Sliding closer to the door so she could see her grandmother, she looked at her pleadingly, "Can we keep one of them, Grandma?" Penny implored. "Please, please?"

"Honey, we're taking them to their forever homes. We aren't allowed to keep any of the dogs we transport."

"Oh please," Penny repeated but this time with less conviction, already knowing the answer. She stuck a finger into the crate to touch the little dog's nose. A tiny pink tongue popped out and licked the tip of her finger. "Aww," Penny crooned softly. "Which one is this," she asked Roy.

"Let's see," he responded looking at his run-sheet. "That one is Polly. She's the lightest color and the friendliest."

"If I could have one, I'd want this one," she said as she petted the dog's nose through the crate.

"Just think how disappointed the family would be that's expecting them this afternoon."

"I guess," she said looking disheartened. Turning toward Sophie and suddenly looking hopeful she asked, "Can I ride in the back with them?"

"You sure may. In fact, we'll tether them to the safety hook in the back so they won't have to get into a crate." That seemed to totally satisfy Penny and she told the pilot they were ready to take them.

Roy opened the kennel door, snapped their leashes on, and carried them down to the tarmac. Penny hurried out of the plane behind him, took both leases, and ran to the grassy area near the fence with the regal little pups at her side. Sophie saw her immediately plop down on the ground while the dogs climbed up on her. She could see the look of excited exhilaration on her granddaughter's face. "There's hope," she said silently to no one.

Roy handed Sophie the dogs' health certificates. She then signed off on the transfer and thanked him for bringing the puppies to Middletown. She and Penny watched him take off into the sky with his precious cargo, headed toward his next delivery.

The roar caused the dogs to tense up and they snuggled closer to Penny. "I think they love me," she said with a touch of sadness in her voice. Sophie wondered if she should talk to Tim about getting a small dog for the girl. She knew Penny loved Emma, and she had even thought about letting her take the dog when she and her father moved to their new house, but she knew she could never part with her Emma.

That's what I'll do, Sophie told herself. *I'll talk to Tim about finding her a dog of her own.*

* * *

Charles could hear his cell phone ringing but wasn't sure where he left it. The sound seemed to be coming from the closet. Suddenly he remembered sliding the phone into his coat pocket when he was walking Barney. He had tried to reach the detective in Buckner to see if he'd made any progress.

By the time he found the phone, it had stopped ringing. He checked the missed calls listing and read, "Buckner WV."

"Must have been Bartlett," he muttered as he hit redial.

"Bartlett."

"Charles Parker here. Say, man, do you have a first name?"

"They just call me Bartlett, or sometimes Bart. Ma gave me a first name, but I used to get beat up for it, so now I'm just 'Bartlett.'" Both men chortled, privately recalling their boyhood days.

"So, Bartlett," Charles began. "What do you have for me?"

"Well, first of all, I needed to get this timeline straight. Let me run it past you now."

"Okay."

"The old guy, Earl Hawkins, left here in 1990. He left a son here who was forty at the time and a grandson, Travis, who was 10."

"Right," Charles responded, but then asked, "And Travis' mother?"

"Travis' mother ran off and left the father to raise the boy alone."

"That brings us to the two unsavory guys you asked me to check out, Darryl and Billy Upton, who turned out to be brothers."

"Did you find out about their connection to Travis?"

"Yeah," Bartlett responded. "Travis' father died not long after his wife left him, possibly suicide, but no one knows for sure. Travis was about fifteen then. The boy went to live with the Upton's on the next farm. There was some sort of loose relationship, like cousins by marriage or something like that. The Upton's boys, Darryl and Billy, never amounted to much but Travis stayed in school, got into computers, and was doing really well. Too bad about that accident. He might have amounted to something…"

"Tell me about Darryl and Billy. What are they doing now?"

"They just did odd jobs around, but they're both gone now."

"Gone? Gone where?" Charles asked with enthusiasm. Maybe our imposter has been identified, he thought hopefully.

"Nobody knows. Their mother, Mrs. Upton, said she doesn't know where either of the boys are and actually didn't seem to care much. Sounds like they caused her a boat-load of trouble over the years. Do you want me to keep looking?"

"Yeah," Charles responded. "I need to know where they are so I can be sure they weren't here. One of them could have been pretending to be Travis Hawkins."

"Yeah. They would have known the right answers…"

"On the other hand," Charles added, "I don't know if an Upton kid could be a good enough actor. The guy that was here pretending to be Travis wasn't someone I'd refer to as unsavory. Aside from the heavy drinking, he seemed to be pretty well put together."

"Where does this leave us?" Bartlett asked.

Charles took a deep breath. "Why don't you nose around and see if you can find out where the Upton brothers went. That way I might have some idea what I'm dealing with."

Chapter 22

"Are you sure no one's here?"

"Well, there are no cars around," Charles responded. "I think it's safe to assume no one is inside. Besides, at the moment, the house doesn't have an owner so if anyone's here, they're trespassing."

"Like we are," Sarah responded as they approached the front door. "How are we getting in?"

"Kirkland gave me a copy of the key our imposter gave him during the fake sale." Charles unlocked the door and opened it to the stale smell of cigarettes. Charles moved quickly through the house, checking the only other rooms -- the bedroom and bath.

"All Clear," he announced in his official tone winking at his lovely partner.

"Where shall we start?" Sarah asked as she opened the back door hoping a cross ventilation would help with the stale air.

"We're looking for papers, documents, anything that might be a clue to who this guy is." Charles headed for the trash can, but it was empty. He was disappointed. It had been his experience that criminals, often not the brightest crayon in the box, would sometimes toss incriminating evidence into the trash.

After checking all the obvious places the imposter might have left something behind, Charles turned to Sarah. "I think the stuff here probably all belonged to the old man."

"I agree, but let's look anyway."

They headed for the bedroom and Charles opened the top dresser drawer. "This guy was a real slob," he said as he rummaged through the hodgepodge of clothing, bills, envelopes, newspaper clippings, and a few packs of cigarettes. The other three drawers were the same. "I wonder how he knew which drawer to open when he wanted socks?"

Charles pulled out all the non-clothing items and placed them on the bare mattress – the only clear surface in the room. "We'll go through this stuff later," he said as he headed for the closet. The closet was essentially empty with only a couple of jackets hanging, along with a very old and tattered black suit. "His funeral attire I assume," Charles muttered. There was a sealed shoebox shoved to the back of the closet that he added to the items on the bed.

Sarah had already started going through the loose items. "These are all utility bills. I'll set them aside." As Charles was looking through the items on the bed, she added, "I found a bunch of letters from Kirkland."

"Let's take a look."

Sarah handed a pile of envelopes to Charles. "These have already been opened. There are more here that are still sealed. Shall I open them?"

"Hold off until I take a look at these," he responded, glancing over the letters one by one. Sarah watched as he placed each one back into its envelope, setting it aside in its original order.

"These are mostly attempts to get old Earl to meet with him," he finally remarked. "Let's take a look at the unopened ones." He carefully opened the first one with his pocket knife, while attempting to preserve any finger prints that might have survived.

A few minutes later he said, "This is interesting," and he began to read. "We have made numerous attempts to reach you, but without success. During our one face-to-face meeting in November you made it clear that the Kirkland offer was unacceptable, but you suggested there might be a figure you could consider. Subsequent figures have been proposed in my previous correspondence, but your silence suggests none of these offers meet with your approval. I appreciate that you understand the value of your property, and I anticipate that together we can arrive at a mutually beneficial figure. I am now requesting that you suggest the next number and I can assure you that Kirkland Enterprises will give it due consideration. Until then, yours truly, etc.'"

"That letter was never opened," Sarah commented. "Hawkins probably didn't know this."

"They might have reached him by phone," Charles speculated. "At any rate, we know he never agreed to sell."

"What about these other letters?" she asked.

"Just hold them aside. I need to think about whether I should be opening them. I probably need a court order. I'll talk to Matt. What else did you find?"

"Just the bills and his checkbook. Do you want to look at that?"

"Not right now. Let's take a look in this box." Again pulling out his pocket knife, Charles reached for the sealed shoe box but then hesitated. "If I need a court order to open those letters, I sure need it for this box. I'm going to call Matt first." He put the shoebox back on the closet floor while Sarah returned the Kirkland correspondence to the top dresser drawer. "Let's head on out of here for now."

* * *

"What do you mean 'shut down?'" Charles asked, sounding bewildered. "You authorized this investigation just last week."

"It's the chief, Charlie. He turned down my request to contract with you on this one."

"So I'll do it for nothing, Matt, if it's a matter of money."

"The chief doesn't want this case reopened."

"This case specifically?"

145

"That's what he said."

"That doesn't make sense. Is he getting pressure from somewhere?"

"That's my guess. He just said 'leave it alone' and he added that if you're available to work, he'd like you assigned to the east side murders. You saw the papers this morning, right?"

"No, I left home early. What is it?" Charles asked apprehensively.

"Another one of our east side senior citizens was attacked in his home. It was another brutal one, Charlie," he added with a tone of despair.

Charles shook his head sorrowfully without speaking for a few moments. Finally he spoke up saying, "Then that's where the pressure is coming from."

"The papers are full of it and the community's in an uproar," Matt responded. "My phone is ringing off the hook; I can just imagine what's going on in the Chief's office."

Later at dinner, Sarah noticed Charles was picking at his food and uncommonly quiet. "Are you okay?" she asked.

"Yes, I guess. I just..." he hesitated but then continued. "You'll see it in the paper anyway, so I might as well tell you. There's been another murder in town – another senior citizen."

"Oh my," she responded laying her fork down. They both sat quietly. Again, he was unwilling to share the details of the brutality so he moved the topic to the Hawkins case.

"He closed us down. The Chief doesn't want time being spent on a closed case when this is going on."

"Do they want you to work the east side cases?"

"I think so."

"Will that be dangerous?"

"No. If they use me at all, they'll only be assigning me to the legwork, like talking to neighbors, looking for possible information, you know the drill – nothing dangerous."

146

Sarah looked relieved but then said, "What about the Hawkins case?"

"There is no case."

"And?"

"And I intend to keep looking."

"On your own?"

"On my own."

"Will you tell Matt?"

"Nope."

"Is that advisable?"

"Well, at least we won't need a search warrant to open that box."

"That's legal?"

"Nope."

"But you'll do it anyway?"

"Absolutely. Old man Hawkins deserves it."

Chapter 23

When Sheila from the shuttle service called the next morning, she requested that Sophie transport a little Papillion mix who was being adopted by a family in New York. "She's been at the Keesler home for several months. You'll be picking her up there and driving her to Smithfield, near the state line. Do you mind traveling that far?"

"No, I'm free today and it's a beautiful day."

"Good. You'll be meeting Joanna Smith who's taking the next leg. Little Magnolia still has a long way to go."

"Have you sent the run-sheet?"

"Yes, I emailed it to you just a few minutes ago."

"Email," Sophie grumbled as she hung up. She had told everyone who would listen that she would never use a computer and here she was doing a job that required her to receive her instructions electronically. "Humph," she grunted aloud. "At least I didn't buy one," she said still speaking aloud. Emma's ears twitched as she tried to catch a word she understood. Charles had offered to loan Sophie his computer and printer until Maria returned from Italy.

"Having a computer," she said looking directly at Emma, "was never the problem. Using it was what I was trying to avoid." Emma wagged her tail.

Charles had taught her how to access her new email account and how to print out the run-sheets. He then prepared her a cheat-sheet, writing down all the steps for accessing and printing the run-sheet. He then prepared a second page of steps describing exactly how to write and send an email. "Just write one to Sarah for practice. You just might like it," he had said.

Sophie printed the run-sheet and looked it over before grabbing her coat and heading out. Emma began crying the minute she sensed that Sophie was leaving. Sophie bent down and took the dog's face between her hands and said, "I'd take you if I could, my dear little furry friend, but it's against the rules. I'll be back as soon as I can." Emma moved closer and pressed her cheek against Sophie's and gently licked her cheek. "I love you too," Sophie whispered.

Although it was extremely cold, the snow had been cleared away on the major roads and Sophie was enjoying the warm sunshine pouring through the windshield. She was glad to be picking Magnolia up from Bernice Keesler. She hadn't met Bernice but knew that she ran a very specialized foster home. She only accepted pregnant dogs, and she cared for them until their pups were due. Bernice then helped the new mothers through the delivery process and lovingly cared for the babies until they were old enough to be adopted.

When Sophie arrived at the Keesler home, she was met at the door by a smiling woman in her mid-fifties. She was carrying a small dog whom she introduced as Magnolia. "We call her Maggie," she added lovingly. "Come on in and have a cup of coffee before you get on the road. You have a long way to go."

Sophie followed her into the kitchen and Bernice handed her the little dog. "Will you hold her while I pour the coffee? It's all ready."

"How adorable," Sophie commented. "It must be hard to say goodbye to these dogs after you've spent so much time with them."

"Very special time," Bernice said. "We've been through a great deal together. Maggie had trouble during the delivery. I had to call in the vet to help us. We thought for a while we were going to lose the puppies, but they all made it."

"What do you know about her background," Sophie asked.

"When they brought Magnolia to me she was covered with fleas, starving, and very pregnant. She had been abandoned by the side of the road along with her crate that had been left open. She had crawled into the crate and patiently waited for her owners to come back for her which, of course, they never did. Judging by her condition, they figured she'd been there for several days." Bernice began to tear up as she told the story.

"Just two weeks after arriving, the babies arrived. She was very weak and malnourished but she got those babies out into the world and has taken excellent care of them."

"She'll miss them," Sophie said softly.

"I insist that pups stay with the mother for at least twelve weeks. Some people let them go earlier, but I like for them to stay with the dam. She does much of the early training and I think it helps her get past that period where they are her whole world."

"And you have a good home for Magnolia?"

"Oh yes. I'm very happy with this family and there was quite a demand for her. Maggie's picture was posted on the website and within twenty-four hours there were a dozen applicants wanting to adopt her. I chose the family in New York because I had a good feeling about them. I think they'll give loving care to this dear little girl." She reached over and petted Magnolia and the dog wiggled so hard Sophie could barely hang onto her.

"Here, let me take her so you can drink your coffee."

"The run-sheet says she's a Papillion mix," Sophie said, not able to take her eyes off the adorable little dog.

"Yes and I'm sure they're right. They call a Papillion the butterfly dog because their fringed ears resemble a butterfly's out-stretched wings. See?" she said as she stretched the ears out.

"I see that," Sophie said enthusiastically. "What do you suppose she's mixed with?"

"I don't know, maybe some Maltese. She has this black button-tipped nose and her hair is pretty long."

"She's a beautiful dog. I'll bet her puppies were adorable.

"I still have one of them if you'd like to see her. Two have been adopted and have gone to their forever homes. The one I still have is pending adoption and she'll probably be picked up tomorrow. I'm going to bring her up with me tonight. I know she'll be lonesome."

Sophie followed Bernice through the house and into what Bernice called the Puppy Room. "This is our little Blossom," Bernice said pointing to a tiny little puppy who immediately dissolved into one big wiggle. "You can pick her up if you want."

Sophie bent down with difficulty but was determined to get her hands on that little soft bundle of fur. Blossom's hair was white and silky with black ears and a touch of black on her back. Her nose was thin and pointy with a tiny black tip, and she had big round brown eyes that looked up at Sophie with anticipation. Blossom stretched to full length and licked Sophie's chin with her tiny pink tongue.

"Don't make me fall in love with you," Sophie pleaded. "Your new mommy will be coming soon."

Sophie felt an empty place in her heart as she drove away from the Keesler house. She looked at Bernice and knew she probably often felt the same.

* * *

"I'm not as comfortable as I was last time we were here," Sarah was saying as they closed the cabin door behind them and headed for the bedroom.

"We'll work fast and get out," Charles assured her. "You take the letters and I'll do the box. Just scan through them and see if there's any new information from Kirkland. Did you bring your gloves?"

"Yes, I remembered." Sarah pulled on the rubber gloves and removed the packet of letters from the dresser drawer. Meanwhile, Charles pulled the box out of the closet and used his pocket knife to cut the tape.

They both worked quietly, neither finding anything of any interest for the first twenty minutes or so. Then Charles spoke up. "I just found the divorce papers."

Sarah looked up with interest and joined him on the edge of the bed. "What does it say?"

"He's the defendant so she filed for the divorce. Let's see, it say the grounds were irreconcilable differences…'irretrievable breakdown of the marriage'…'past efforts failed.'" Charles thumbed through the pages and returned to the second page. "It says they lived 'separate and apart' since May 1992…" Turning back to the last page, "This was finalized in 2011."

"She sure waited a long time to get the divorce – nearly twenty years," Sarah noted. "There must be an interesting story there."

"We'll probably never know." Picking up the contents of the box, Charles returned them and placed the box back in the closet. "Did you find anything in the letters?"

"No, just the same thing we read in the first letters. It doesn't look like Hawkins ever spoke with Kirkland after that initial meeting."

"Wait a minute, Charles. Something fell on the floor." She reached to pick it up. "It looks like another legal document. She handed it to Charles and waited while he opened it. "What is it?" she asked when she saw his face change.

"It's his will," Charles responded with disbelief. "Why didn't anyone find this?"

"I doubt that anyone was looking," Sarah responded. "Who would have looked?"

Charles began reading. "Good Lord," he exclaimed. "This document leaves everything to the grandson, Travis Hawkins."

Chapter 24

"Ladies, I think we may have enough dog house blocks. Let's take a break and count them."

"We have twenty-one," Christina called out a few minutes later. "How many do we need?"

"Well, we have several different sizes and I'm not sure just how we'll be laying them out, but I think we'll probably need about four across and five down. That would be twenty, but we might need more. Let's stop and decide how we want to arrange them."

"Since we have varying sizes, we can use wider strips of sashing to fill the space where we need it," Delores suggested.

"I don't get it," Sophie muttered, not intending for anyone to hear her.

"You will," Ruth assured her confidently. "Just wait and see."

Sarah held up the sashing fabric they had chosen the previous week, which was black with light blue, yellow, and tan paw prints scattered on it. "This is what we decided to use as sashing between the blocks. Let's wait to choose our borders after we finish the middle."

"How big will this be?" Caitlyn asked. She rarely asked questions, being the youngest in the group and the least experienced. A slight blush spread across her cheeks.

Sarah encouraged her by responding, "I'm glad you asked. We need to talk about that. As it stands now, it would probably only be about 55"x75" once we add a couple of borders. We could always make more blocks and increase the size. What do you think?" she added, addressing the whole group.

"I like for a throw to be bigger than that," Delores responded. As the oldest member and most experienced, the group turned toward her to hear her suggestion. "How about we frame each of the blocks using the three colors in the sashing: blue, yellow, and tan. That will give us another sixteen or so inches all the way around. That would be a generous size."

"It could even fit a child's twin bed if the winner wanted to use it that way."

"Let's do it," Ruth responded. "Come into the shop and we'll find our three fabrics."

While they were searching through the shop, Sarah turned to Sophie and asked, "Are you still upset about Penny bringing a boy over?"

"No, Andy explained it to me. It's how kids study nowadays. In fact, he's driving a bunch of kids to the movies on Saturday. It's some movie their history teacher recommended. Andy said it will be good for her to get to know these kids – it's a group who are concerned about their studies and their grades. In fact, Andy said the boy Penny brought home is in an advanced college-prep program."

"It sounds like this has worked out just fine," Sarah said. "What do you think of this fabric?" she asked Sophie pulling out a bolt of brown tone-on-tone.

Sophie was holding a piece of the black sashing fabric. She held it up to the bolt and said, "I think it should be a lighter tan. This one will fade into the black."

"Good point," Sarah agreed returning the bolt.

"How about this one?" Sophie said as she pulled out another tone-on-tone. "It has a touch of gold to it, but it will stand out better."

"I totally agree," Sarah said again. "You're really good with color." They carried the golden tan up to the cutting table and laid it down next to the other candidates.

"That's perfect," several women said simultaneously as they removed the other tan bolts. The yellow and blue choices were already made. By the time all three fabrics were cut into strips and sewn onto each of the twenty blocks, it was approaching nine o'clock.

"Let's go ahead and clean up," Ruth announced. "They're predicting snow again tonight, and I'd like for everyone to get home before it starts."

Sophie had been pressing all the blocks and had them neatly stacked and ready to be sewn into rows. Sarah gathered up the blocks and the sashing fabric. She had offered to take them home and add the sashing strips to save time. "I might even go ahead and sew the rows together if I have time," she had added.

As they were preparing to leave, Delores picked up the one extra block and said, "I'd be happy to use my embroidery machine to make a label using this block if someone tells me what it should say."

"It should say it was made by the Running Stitches Friday Night Quilters," Ruth said.

"And add our home town."

"And the date..."

"That's fine, but doesn't it need something else?"

Sophie was standing nearby thumbing through the quilt books. She turned toward the group and said, "I saw a poster recently with the picture of an adorable little dog and under the picture it said, 'I am not disposable. Please love me for my whole life.'"

The group was obviously touched and remained quiet for a moment until Delores finally spoke up. Her voice cracked slightly as she said, "That's the perfect message for our rescue quilt." Everyone shook their heads in agreement. Caitlyn had tears in her eyes as she reached over and gently touched Sophie's arm.

* * *

"How are things going with Penny?" Charles asked, peeking into the sewing room where Sarah appeared to be lost in thought.

"We've practically finished her quilt and she's a natural with that machine."

"I thought she was just going to be watching."

"She wanted to try sewing a seam. It was perfectly straight and she understood about the quarter-inch seam, so she actually did much of the stitching. We finished it yesterday, and we're taking it to the quilter next week."

"And how about your ulterior motive? Has she opened up with you?"

"More and more every day. Caitlyn was right; that girl needs to talk. I think she'd do great in counseling and I'm going to suggest it to Tim one of these days, but I want to introduce the topic to her first."

"But she is talking to you, right?"

"She is, but I'm sure there's more she'd like to talk about. Sometimes I think she's holding back. Other times she's told me things I'd almost rather not know."

"How's that?" he asked sitting down on a chair near the worktable where she had dog house blocks spread out. It was one of the many things she loved about her husband. When she talked to him she could tell that she had his total attention. She wondered how often she continued working on things while half listening to her friends. She was learning from Charles how important it is to stop and really hear what people are saying.

"Things weren't all sunshine and roses back in Alaska. I know her mother was sick for a long time, but it sounds like she got pretty difficult toward the end."

"I've heard that can happen with cancer."

"It was actually more than just being difficult," Sarah added looking distressed. "The mother became abusive at times."

156

"Oh the poor child, and I'm sure she didn't understand what was happening."

"She wonders what she was doing wrong," Sarah replied. "I've tried to help her see that it didn't have anything to do with her, but she can't see that."

"And the mother probably didn't have anyone but Penny to care for her."

"No, just Penny. It was a very hard time for the young girl." Sarah was haphazardly moving the blocks around on the worktable. Realizing what she was doing, she pushed them aside and turned to Charles. "Remember when Caitlyn told me that Penny wanted to go back home?"

"Yes, but surely she knew there was no home there..." Charles responded.

"Of course she knew. I don't think that's what she really wanted. After talking with her, I think she wanted to do the impossible – she wanted to go back in time and apologize for being angry with her mother. She told me it was hard to be patient with her some of the time."

"Hmm. The woman was probably in unbearable pain. I wonder what kind of medical care she had."

"Penny said it was impossible to get her mother to the doctor's office toward the end. Actually he went to the cabin a time or two, but her mother often ran out of medication. That was really too much for a young girl."

Charles shook his head. "I wish she had contacted Tim earlier. He would have helped. He's a good guy."

"Well, at least she finally did let him know about Penny. I hate to think where she'd be today without Tim."

"And now Penny has a good home and is with family that loves her," Charles added on a more positive note.

"True, but unfortunately that seems to be the other part of the problem. She told me she feels like she's imposing on Tim and Sophie."

"Imposing? Those two are happy as clams! They love that girl."

"We know that, but Penny doesn't. She knows she has changed their lives -- she just doesn't realize they are changed for the better. They are both ecstatic about having her in the family. I've tried to help her see that. I think it'll just take time.

"Do we need to worry about her taking off for Alaska?"

"Absolutely not," Sarah responded. "She understands now that going back isn't the solution. She wants to stay right where she is. She just wants to fit in."

"And, as you said, that'll take time," Charles said. "I'm glad you're working with her. The more support she has, the better."

Sarah turned to the worktable and took four blocks off the pile of finished squares.

"What are you working on there?"

"I offered to put the rows together, but I forgot that would involve figuring out where to place each of the dog house blocks. I think I'll put them all on the design wall you made for me. Will you help me put it up?"

"Sure thing." He moved closer to her worktable and studied each of the blocks. "These are terrific. It's going to be raffled off, right?"

"Yes. Sophie spoke with the organization and they're planning a city-wide raffle. It'll be advertised in the paper and they got approval from the county to display it and sell tickets at the spring craft show at the fair ground."

"This should bring in good money. It's going to be very unique," Charles responded. "Am I allowed to buy tickets?" he asked in a somewhat teasing tone.

"You're allowed to buy as many tickets as you want," she responded cheerfully. "But I'm not sure we'd allow you to keep it if you win."

"What? That's not fair," he said, looking injured.

"Sometimes life just isn't fair," she teased. "We've agreed that if any of us in the club should happen to win, we'll donate it back and I'm pretty sure that applies to you as well."

Chapter 25

Sophie picked up the phone on the second ring. She could see it was a call from the Shuttle Service and she hoped Sheila didn't have a run for her today. She wanted to help Penny with her packing. She and her father were moving to their new home today and it was bittersweet for Sophie. She was happy for them as they began their new life, but it had been wonderful having family in the house. She knew they were just up the street, and Penny promised she would come by after school most afternoons, but not having her to tuck into bed at night was indeed sad.

"Sophie, glad I caught you. I just had a call from the Keesler foster home. You were out there the other day picking up Magnolia."

"I remember. Is there a problem?"

"No, not at all. In fact, I heard that Magnolia has settled into her new home and is happy as a clam. The reason Bernice Keesler was calling was because of one of Magnolia's babies. She said you seemed to be interested in her, but she was in the process of being adopted."

"Oh yes, I remember that little sweetie. Her name is Blossom and she was so adorable. I felt like she was asking me to take her home. Actually, I would have if it had been possible."

"Well," Sheila continued, "You're in luck. The adoption didn't go through and little Blossom is available. I'll give you Bernice's number and you can go fill out an application if you're still interested. How will Emma feel about having another dog in the family?"

"Actually, I was thinking about getting her for my granddaughter."

160

"Oh," Sheila replied hesitantly. "Does she live with you?"

"She's been living here, but she and her father are packing to move to their new home that is just up the street..."

"Sophie, you'll have to have her father fill out the application. They'll do the home study at the new house. Do you know if there's a fenced yard?"

"Yes, as a matter of fact. And Penny is fourteen. She'll take excellent care of the little dog. She loves Emma and spends every available minute playing with her."

"I know she will. And besides, she's your granddaughter. I know she'll do fine. Give Bernice a call after you talk to your son and perhaps the three of you can go meet little Blossom just to make sure this is the dog for Penny."

This is the perfect dog for Penny – a little white bundle of fluff to love, Sophie thought. "We'll give Bernice a call. Thanks Sheila."

"Tell your son to give me as one of his references when he fills out the forms." Tim had been helping Sophie with her runs and had made an impression on Sheila. "Such a fine young man," she had said despite the fact that he was almost as old as Sheila.

Sophie hung up and remained sitting on the couch thinking about the little dog. She had hoped to get Penny a dog as a surprise, but she was beginning to realize that this was best. Penny should be involved in choosing the dog. Who knows what attracts certain dogs and humans to one another, but she remembered that when she met Emma they seemed to have a special connection from the beginning.

"Yes," she told herself aloud, "Penny needs to meet little Blossom."

* * *

All plans for moving their clothes to the new house came to a grinding halt when Sophie told Penny and Tim about little

Blossom. "I'll drive," Tim announced. "You two can hold the dog."

"Hold on son. We won't be bringing the dog home with us today."

"Why not?" Penny cried in a whiney voice Sophie hadn't heard her use before.

"Because they have to do a home study. Remember how I was telling you that they always make sure the dogs are going to a good home."

"But we are a good home," she protested.

"Of course we are, but they don't know that."

"You could tell them..." Penny grumbled.

"Just be patient, young lady," Sophie responded, trying to sound firm while smiling inside. She realized that Penny was becoming comfortable enough in her new home to begin to grouse occasionally, and she knew that was a very good thing.

As they drove toward the Keesler home, Penny became animated again asking questions about the dog and talking about all the things they would need to buy.

"Can we buy a bed today?" she asked her father.

"Don't worry," he replied. "We'll get everything we need before she arrives." Turned to Sophie, he asked, "Mom, how long do these home studies usually take?"

"I'm not sure. By the time I get involved, the adoptions are already done, but I think it will go quickly since they know us, and Sheila has offered to provide a personal reference."

As they were approaching the front door, Bernice Keesler stepped out and greeted them. "I'm so glad you're still interested. I could tell when you were here, you were really bonding with little Blossom."

Sophie introduced Tim and Penny and the four went into the house and headed immediately for the puppy room. When they stepped into the room, Penny gasped and covered her face with both hands. "Is that her?" she asked almost afraid to hear the answer in case it wasn't Blossom.

"That's little Blossom," Bernice said, picking her up and gently handing her to Penny.

"Ooh, she's so little and soft." Penny held her close to her heart and kissed the top of her head. "I love her," she said softly. Blossom stretched up just like she had done with Sophie and licked Penny's chin with her tiny pink tongue.

"Ah," Penny cooed. "Look at these big ears," she said gently running her hand across the back of the puppy's shiny black ears. The black area on her back was more pronounced and she had grown since Sophie saw her, but she was still tiny and appeared to be ever so delicate. "I'm afraid I'll break her," Penny said as she carefully put her back into her bed. "When can I take her home?" she abruptly asked, catching Bernice off guard.

"Oh, well, there's a procedure. We'll do a home study. I understand you're in the process of moving. How soon do you expect to be settled?" she asked turning to Tim.

"We're already settled," he said knowing that they only had one more trip to make with a few clothes and they'd be completely moved in.

"Then why don't I give you the application to complete. Get it back to me as soon as you can, and I'll schedule the home visit right away." She led them back to the kitchen and pulled out a packet. "Just complete this and bring it back to me."

"Can we bring it back today?" Penny asked.

"Hold on, young lady," Tim responded. "This will take some time and it's already afternoon but," he added turning to Bernice, "I think we can get it back to you tomorrow if that's okay."

"That's fine. I'll see you then."

"May I go say goodbye to Blossom?" Penny asked as they were heading toward the front door.

Bernice laughed and said, "Of course you may."

When Penny came running back toward the front door, she had a broad grin. "She kissed me again."

Chapter 26

Bernice was coming back to the living room, having toured the entire house except for the basement. "Blossom won't be going down there," Tim had assured her. "In fact, I doubt that any of us will be going down there," he added. "It's cold and damp and I don't trust those steps."

"This is a nice little house for the two of you and, with that fenced yard, Blossom will have a great place to play. I checked for holes where she might escape and didn't find any, but I suggest that you go out with her the first few times and make sure she doesn't find them herself. She's pretty small."

"Does this mean we can get her?" Tim asked. Penny was still in school and he hadn't told her about the home visit, knowing she wouldn't be able to concentrate on her lessons all day.

"Absolutely. Sheila called me with her reference. She is very impressed with you and all the help you've been to the Shuttle Service. And, of course, your mother has been an angel. They're hoping she continues with the program after her friend Maria returns."

"Yes, I'm sort of torn on that. She's getting up in years and I hate to think of her driving all over the countryside, but some of the time I'm able to be with her and sometimes she takes Penny along. Actually, Mom even has friends that like to ride along. I do know it's brought her a great deal of joy. She really loves tooling around in her Pup Mobile and when she comes home she always says 'well, I saved another life today.'"

They both chuckled, and then Bernice said, "So, do you want to come pick up Blossom, or do you want to have her delivered?"

"I'd love to bring Penny and pick her up. When can we come?"

"How about tomorrow?"

"We'll be there," he responded, knowing how excited Penny would be when she heard.

"Here's a list of some of the things you'll need including the food she's been eating. I'll give you her medical records when you come to pick her up. She's current on everything and in excellent health. She's an adorable little dog," she added wistfully. "I'll miss her."

"You must get very attached."

"I do, but it always makes me happy when I see them go to a good home. And I know Blossom is going to be loved."

"She absolutely will be," he responded, realizing that at that moment he was happier than he had ever been in his life.

When Penny got home from school that afternoon, she found her father with a big grin on his face.

"What's going on?" she asked.

"We can pick up little Blossom tomorrow morning. She's all yours!"

Penny jumped up and down with excitement. "Can't we go right now, please Daddy. Pu-leese." Tim's smile grew even wider hearing his daughter calling him 'daddy' and seeing her happier than she had been in several months.

"I wish we could, sweetie, but we'll go first thing in the morning...well, actually we'll go second thing in the morning. First of all, we need to go to the pet store and stock up on food and a few other things."

"Can't we go do that now? That way we can get up real early and go get her."

Tim laughed and reached over to hug his daughter. For the first time, she relaxed into his hug and gently leaned against his chest. "Thank you, Daddy. I love Blossom so much!"

166

"I know," he responded patiently. "And she loves you. In fact we all love you!"

Penny leaned back and looked up at her father. There was love in her eyes that she couldn't express yet, but Tim could see it. "We all love you," he repeated. "Now put your coat back on – we have some shopping to do."

When they entered the store, Penny hurried to the dog section and by the time Tim got there she had an armload of toys. "Hold on," he said. "Let's not overwhelm the little girl. How about picking out your five favorite toys. I'll go get a shopping cart."

Eliminating toys took time. "These are all my favorites," she mumbled at one point, but was finally able to reduce the pile to seven. "See, this one squeaks and this one is soft and furry like her mommy. She'll love that one. And this one..."

"Okay, okay," Tim chuckled. "Put all seven in the cart."

"Basket!" Penny cried. "She needs a basket for her toys."

"We'll stop at the craft store for that. They have lots of baskets..."

"And she needs a basket to sleep in..." Penny ran up the aisle. "I saw some over here." She stopped at the deep shelves on the wall and stared at all the beds. "I don't know which one she'd like," she said, looking perplexed. "These all look too big."

"How about these over here," Tim suggested leading her to a section of much smaller beds. He picked up a brown one and pointed to the front. "It's very low here and she'll be able to get in and out easily."

"And it's very soft," Penny said, but sounded hesitant.

"Don't you like it?" Tim asked.

"Well..."

She turned back to the shelf and dug throw the array of small beds until she saw what she was looking for. "There it is, back there," she said excitedly. "Can you reach it?" She wasn't exactly jumping up and down, but Tim saw that she was bouncing with excitement. "That's it," she repeated.

"The pink one?" he asked, stretching across the shelf for the pink furry bed in the very back.

"Yes. Yes. That's it." She was now hopping around with excitement. "It's perfect."

Mom was right. This dog is exactly what my girl needed to pull her out of her shell, Timothy thought.

"What else do we need?" Penny asked as she carefully placed the bed into the shopping cart.

Tim pulled out the list Bernice had given him and headed for the food aisle. "Here it is," he said, starting to pick up a bag.

"That says it's for adult dogs, Daddy. Shouldn't she have this one?" She held up a smaller bag, which was labeled "Puppy."

"You're absolutely right. Stick that one in the cart."

Penny carefully lifted the pink fluffy bed out in order to put the food in. "I didn't want to crush it," she explained when she noticed her father was watching her.

From there, they picked up two very small dishes for Blossom's food and water, chose a bag of small training treats, and looked at collars and leashes. "What size should we get?" Penny asked looking confused by all the sizes.

"I have an idea," Tim responded. "Let's stop here tomorrow after we pick her up and try them on her."

"We can bring her into the store?"

"It says on the door dogs are welcome as long as they're on leashes. We can carry her in. They'll understand."

"Look," Penny said as they were approaching the checkout counter. "It's a machine for making a name tag. Can I make one that says "Blossom?"

"Sure, and let's put our new phone number on it just in case she gets out."

On their way to the car, both loaded down with bags, Tim said, "I noticed a sign that said they offer training classes. Would you like to do that with her when she's bigger?"

"Oh yes, I'd love that."

They stopped for pizza on their way home, and talked with excitement about picking up little Blossom the next morning.

* * *

"I don't know how good I'll be tonight with that iron. I'm so excited I can't stop giggling." On the way to the quilt club, Sophie told Sarah that Tim and Penny would be picking up their dog the next morning. "Penny called me to tell me about all the things they got at the pet store and she wanted me to ask you something."

"What's that?" Sarah asked.

"She's wondering if you'll help her made a quilt for Blossom. She wants to make it in pink to match the bed they bought today."

Sarah laughed. "Of course I will. Here, take my phone and call her. I want to speak to her." As Sophie dialed, Sarah pulled over to the curb and parked in front of the quilt shop.

"Hi Penny," Sarah heard Sophie say. "Yes, I just told her and she wants to talk to you." Sophie handed the phone to Sarah.

"Penny, I wanted to let you know that I'd be very happy to help you make a quilt for Blossom. I'm at the fabric store now. Would you like for me to pick up some fabric?" Sophie listened to Sarah's end of the conversation and could tell that Penny was telling her exactly what she had in mind. "Okay, I'll look for pink fabric with puppy dogs and something with flowers. Oh, and you also like green? Okay. I'll see what they have."

When Sarah finished, Sophie took the phone and told Penny how happy she was about the dog. "I can hardly wait to see her."

They had arrived a few minutes early, and there were still customers in the shop. They decided to wait until Ruth hung the "closed" sign before going in.

"How do they like their new home?" Sarah asked.

"Tim's a guy. He doesn't much care where he hangs his hat as long as it has a television and a refrigerator. As for Penny, this little cottage is a mansion. She just keeps marveling at all its conveniences, like hot water and electricity around the clock. Even dependable plumbing. She told me that in the winter she and her mother would make their way through four feet of snow to get to the outdoor facilities."

"The outhouse?" Sarah asked, looking surprised.

"Yes, the outhouse. Can you imagine?"

"What did they do when her mother was too sick to go out?"

"They had plumbing by that time. I understand Penny's grandfather did the work."

"I didn't know she had a grandfather," Sarah responded.

"He died a few years ago. We're her only family. That's why I'm so glad Tim found out about her when he did."

About that time, Kimberly broke the spell by tapping on the window and saying, "You two are going to freeze out here. Hop out of that car and get inside. We're finishing a quilt tonight!"

Sarah and Sophie's moods were immediately brightened when Sarah spread out the center of the quilt all sewn together and ready for borders. The group became animated as they congratulated themselves on a job well done. "Who did that one with two bull dogs?" someone asked.

"That's mine," Allison responded. "And look at this one..."

After a few minutes, Ruth clapped her hands to get their attention. "Okay ladies, let's get down to business. We need to decide about borders. Let's go into the shop and see what looks good.

They tried out several patterns but decided they took away from the dog house blocks. Ruth suggested several tone-on-tone pieces, but the group didn't seem pleased with any of the options.

Finally Sarah spoke up. "I was wondering about using the same fabric we used for the sashing – the paw prints."

"Don't we need something to separate the border from the blocks…"

"How about these dog bones?" Sophie said, holding up a bolt of tone on tone tan with a dog-bone pattern.

"Hmm," Sarah responded, "I like it. We could just use a two-inch piece of the dog bones for an inner border and then a four inch piece of the paw prints for an outer border. What do the rest of you think?"

Everyone agreed and Delores offered to sew the borders on once they were cut.

"While Delores is adding the borders, I'd like to bring up something that's bothering me."

"What is it, Allison?" Ruth asked as the others sat down to listen. Delores stopped working as well.

"This might be silly, but I keep looking at the large areas of sashing. With the blocks being different sizes, we've created some areas that look sort of blank."

"Do you have an idea for what we could do?" Sarah asked.

"Actually, I do. I saw some cat fabric in the shop and I wondered what it would look like if we appliqued a cat here and there."

"Ooh," several quilters responded.

"I like it," Sarah exclaimed. "I have to admit that was bothering me too, but I couldn't think of anything to do about it."

"Is anyone in the group particularly good at applique?" Allison asked. "I'm not good with a needle and thread."

"We could always do machine applique..."

The group discussed it while Ruth went into the shop to find the cat fabric. She returned with two bolts, one with cats of various colors on a white background and another with the same cats on black.

"Here's what we have on hand," Ruth announced. "I would recommend that we use the ones on the black background because they will blend into our sashing, which also has a black background. What do you think?"

"I agree," Sarah said, and the rest of the group nodded their agreement.

"I'm not sure how this is going to look," Delores observed in a worried tone.

"How about this," Kimberly began. "Christina and I are taking the quilt home in order to quilt it. We'll give the applique a try and see how it looks, okay?"

"In fact," Christina added, "I'll bring it into the shop with a few cats appliqued on and you gals can stop in during the day on Wednesday and take a look. Let Ruth know whether or not you like it."

"Majority rules," Ruth added.

The group agreed to the plan, and, while Delores worked on the borders, the rest of the group went through the book of quilting patterns that Kimberly had brought in. They came up with a simple meandering pattern that they felt wouldn't take away from the animals.

"Let's talk about how we'll present the quilt," Sarah said. "I've been wondering about inviting a couple of representatives from the rescue organization to come to a meeting. We could serve refreshments and present the quilt."

"Do you think we could invite the newspaper? It would be great publicity for them and for the raffle," Delores suggested, stopping her machine temporarily to join the discussion.

"...and for the shop!" Ruth responded. "I'll make all the arrangements once Kimberly and Christina finish the quilting."

"We'll still need to add the binding."

"If someone will stitch the binding on by machine, I'd be happy to hem it," Sophie offered.

"Oh wonderful, Sophie," Sarah responded knowing how much Sophie wanted to be involved in the project. "Sophie does excellent handwork," she added.

As they were getting into the Pup Mobile to leave, Sarah noticed a satisfied grin spread across Sophie's face. "That tee-shirt of yours is right," Sophie said. "Life is good."

Chapter 27

"Bartlett. I didn't expect to hear from you today. What's up?"

"Actually Charles, I was just curious about something and thought I'd call and ask. You've never mentioned Earl's other son and I was wondering why he isn't being considered in the mix."

"What other son?"

"The one that was born out there."

"Out here?" Charles was totally confused. "He didn't have another son."

"Oh, I just assumed it was a boy. A girl, huh?"

"Bartlett, what are you talking about?"

"You don't know?" Bartlett responded incredulously.

"I truly don't know what you're talking about. What's going on?"

"Okay. Remember when you asked me to check out old man Hawkins' life before he left West Virginia?"

"I do. Go on."

"Well, there wasn't much on old Earl Hawkins. Most of his generation is gone. I spoke with the son of one of his friends, a Harvey Miller. He said that to his knowledge no one had heard from Earl after he left town with his pregnant wife some twenty-five years ago."

"Pregnant wife?"

"Yep. He'd married some young chick -- Rita something. I haven't been able to pin down her maiden name yet. They took off for Middletown where she had family. Miller said they'd bought a cabin out there."

"To tell you the truth, Bart, I don't know anything about another child. There's got to be some mistake."

A pregnant wife? Charles sat and tried to absorb this new information. *A pregnant wife? This means there may be another heir out there.*

Charles left Sarah a note and took off for City Hall to search the birth records for the years 1990 and 1991. "I'm looking for a child born to an Earl Hawkins," he told the clerk. "The mother's name was Rita, but I don't have her maiden name. They were married so I assume the mother's listed as Rita Hawkins."

"Will do," the clerk responded cheerfully. "It's been a slow day and I welcome any excuse to play with that new computer. I can track this down for you in no time," he bragged.

A few minutes later he returned with a broad smile. "Found it," he announced slapping the printout down on the counter. "Patrick Henry Nichols born on September 29, 1991 to Earl Hawkins and Geraldine Nichols." The clerk grinned with pride for having accomplished the search so quickly.

"Wrong Hawkins," Charles replied feeling annoyed as his temporary euphoria drained away. "Could you check again? The mother's name is Rita, not Geraldine."

"Sorry," the clerk mumbled. "We've got a passel of Hawkins in these parts – three or four pages in the phonebook. I'll check again." A few minutes later, he returned, this time appearing more reticent. "This must be it," he said apologetically handing the printout to Charles. I searched on the mother's name."

"This time you got it right," Charles responded, looking at the document and smiling. "Christopher Hawkins, born August 1, 1990, to Earl and Rita Hawkins."

* * *

"I think I've identified our imposter, Matt, and perhaps even a killer." He slaps the birth certificate down on the lieutenant's desk and stands back looking smug. "Take a look."

Matt picks up the document. "This is a birth certificate," he exclaims frowning and looking perplexed.

"Read the date," Charles responded.

"August 1, 1990. This guy's twenty-five now. Are you saying this is the guy that's been impersonating the grandson?"

"It's my best guess at this point, and he may even be the killer -- assuming Earl Hawkins was actually murdered."

"And just who is this guy?" Looking back at the document he read aloud, "Mother Rita Hawkins, father Earl Hawkins." The puzzled look left his face as he looked up. "So old Earl had another son?"

"You got it. It's my guess that this guy showed up here and found out about the potential estate his father was leaving to his grandson, Travis. He must have killed Hawkins and pretended to be his grandson Travis so he could slip away with the money, and we'd be looking for Travis, not him. He must not have known Travis was dead."

"Killed his own dad? That sounds pretty farfetched to me." The lieutenant looked back at the document. "How did you find out there was another son? And by the way, I thought I took you off this case."

"Bartlett came up with the information and I felt I should follow up."

"Bartlett? He's still working for you?"

"Yeah, Matt. I needed him."

"And you're paying him yourself?"

"Yep. It's still cheaper than travelling to West Virginia."

Matt shook his head and sighed in exasperation. "I guess you're going to do what you're going to do. Fix up an invoice and I'll try to get you reimbursed."

176

"Thanks Matt."

Matt continued to stare at the birth certificate and appeared to be deep in thought. "Tell me, Charlie, those divorce papers you and Sarah found back in the cabin -- What did they say about the kid?"

"Nothing. The papers were dated 2011. The kid was twenty-one by then."

"How about an address on the mother. She'd know where the kid ended up."

"Dead end. It was a dilapidated apartment building that was condemned in 2013. No records on tenants."

"Hmm. So we have nothing."

"We might have his DNA," Charles responded. "The medical examiner is looking at that but it won't be much help unless he's in the system."

"It'll proves he was in the house and Kirkland can identify him as the guy that ripped him off. We could get him on fraud, but we'd be hard pressed to get him on murder unless we get a confession."

"That's all true if we find him," Charles responded and then added with a raised eyebrow, "If we're even looking, that is."

Stokely sighed again and with resignation said, "Go ahead and look, detective. I'll submit the paperwork."

Chapter 28

"Charlie, it's Charlotte Johansson. I have some information I think you'll find very interesting. Give me a call."

Charles had just returned from his meeting with Matt Stokely. He was eager to sit down with Sarah and discuss what he had learned but the message left by the medical examiner was intriguing. He dialed the number she had left.

"Charlotte, it's Charles Parker."

"Charlie, glad you called. I have the DNA results for you."

"And?" he responded hoping she had a name for him.

"He's not in the system, but there's something interesting about it."

"I could use something interesting about now. What is it?"

"The sample you gave me shares a DNA profile with that old man you were asking about earlier, Earl Hawkins."

"Shares a DNA profile? What does that mean?"

"They're related and I'd say they're immediate family, perhaps father and son."

"Excellent! That's just what I wanted to know. Thank you, Charlotte."

"Anytime, Charlie. Sorry it took so long."

"You got it here at exactly the right time. Before today, I wouldn't have known what to do with this information. But now I do. Thanks again," and he hung up the phone with a satisfied smile. "I got you, young man. Now I just have to find you."

* * *

"So you think this younger son is the man who was pretending to be Travis Hawkins?"

"I'm sure of it."

Sarah removed three slices of bacon from the grill, blotted away the excess grease with a paper towel, and arranged them carefully on a slice of toast. She then added a thick slice of tomato, two large lettuce leaves, and a second slice of toast, which had been lightly spread with something that looked like mayonnaise, but that Charles had learned was another imposter. She placed the sandwich on a small plate that she then placed in front of Charles as she removed his soup bowl.

"A BLT?" he responded with astonishment "You're giving me bacon?"

"Turkey bacon, Charles, and I think you'll like it."

He took a cautious bite and raised his left eyebrow. "Not bad..."

"Just 'not bad'?"

"Okay. Actually, it's pretty good." He had promised himself he would stop complaining about his diet, but he occasionally became a bit cranky when he didn't get the fatty, calorie-laden foods he loved. He knew she had changed his diet for his own good and appreciated the effort it took for her to help guide him to a healthier life style. Still, he missed the juicy burgers and delicious desserts he knew she was capable of preparing. He hoped that when his numbers were looking better they could enjoy the occasional exception.

She brought her own sandwich to the table and joined him. "So," she began. "Have you found the young Christopher Hawkins yet?"

"No, but I've located the mother and hopefully she will lead us directly to the son. I'm waiting for the go ahead from Matt before I contact her."

"If this Christopher is Earl Hawkins' son, wouldn't he be entitled to the inheritance? Why would he have to try to trick Kirkland by pretending to sell the property to him?"

"He would have been entitled to it if there hadn't been a will – but there was and as you remember Hawkins left everything to his grandson, Travis."

"I see…but Travis is dead."

"Obviously Christopher didn't know that. He would probably have been next in line for the inheritance if he'd just waited."

"I'd like to go with you," Sarah said trying to keep a lid on her excitement about possibly having the opportunity to be involved in the investigation. She always found it exciting, but Charles often held her back, not wanting to place her in harm's way.

"That might not be a bad idea," he responded, much to her surprise. "You being there just might put the woman more at ease. I can't help but act like a cop when I'm asking questions."

Charles had finished his sandwich and was looking around for something, but he wasn't sure what. Dessert, he suddenly realized but didn't say.

"How about a bit of dessert," his wife said knowing him well enough to know exactly what was on his mind.

"You mean…?" he asked skeptically

Sarah smiled and opened the oven, removing a baking dish with two steaming baked apples.

"I thought I'd been smelling apple pie, but I figured it was just wishful thinking." He dug into the baked apple actually forgetting it was the new healthy version. "This is delicious," he announced with gusto. Sarah smiled to herself.

Chapter 29

"The house is in the next block," Sarah said returning the GPS to the glove box and locking it. It had snowed the previous night leaving a covering of no more than two inches, just enough to cause problems on the road. "That's it right up there on the left."

As they approached the house, they spotted a young man shoveling snow from the sidewalk leading up to the house. His back was to them and he was bundled up in a heavy jacket and cap. Charles pulled up to curb just as the man turned.

"Good Lord," Sarah gasped. "It's him. It's the man pretending to be Travis." She moved closer to Charles. "We should leave," she added nervously. "He could be dangerous."

"I'm not authorized to arrest him but I'll call for backup. You wait here while I..."

The young man was walking toward the car. "Can I help you folks?" he asked with a warm smile as he pulled off his stocking cap and shook his hair into place.

"That's not him," Sarah muttered with a sigh of relief. "It looked like him from a distance, but it's not him."

Charles hit the button and lowered the window on Sarah's side. "Excuse me," he called out. "Is this the Hawkins house?"

"Sure is. I'm Christopher Hawkins. Did you want to see me or my Mother?"

"We'd like to see your mother if she's available," he said trying not to reveal his bewilderment. "You're her son, right?" he asked as he got out of the car and approached the young man.

"Yes sir," he responded. "And you are...?"

Charles pulled out his department identification and introduced himself. "And this is my wife Sarah Parker."

"How do you do, Mrs. Parker," the young man responded, as he opened the passenger door and offered her a hand getting out. "Come on in. I'll let Mom know you're here."

Once Christopher introduced them to his mother, he turned to go back outside. "Call me if you need me, mom."

"Have a seat," she said to Charles and Sarah. "May I offer you anything, coffee perhaps?"

"No thank you," Sarah responded. She then looked toward her husband encouraging him to take charge of the visit. He still looked perplexed.

"Mrs. Hawkins, I'm working with the local police department helping out with investigations and background checks. I have just a few questions for you."

"Please call me Rita. I haven't been Mrs. Hawkins for many years. Is this about Earl's death?"

"Actually," Charles began but wasn't sure where he was going from there. He came to the house hoping to locate her son Christopher, but he had just met Christopher and he wasn't the man Charles was expecting him to be. "Actually," he began again, "I was hoping to ask you a few questions about your ex-husband. I understand he died of a massive heart attack..."

Sarah had to struggle to hide her amusement as she watched Charles attempting to deal with the very awkward situation. He clearly had no idea how to explain their visit since her son, Christopher, was clearly not the person they thought it would be. Pulling herself together, she decided to help him out. "Rita, I know you're wondering why we're here. A dear friend of mine is the one who found your ex-husband and called the police. She called us as well and we were all there at the cabin. It was an upsetting experience for us and we just wanted to touch base with the family and make sure everyone is okay." She smiled sweetly and could see Charles out of the side of her eye as he expelled a deep breath of relief.

"Yes," he added as he relaxed and smiled his appreciation to his wife. "Have the police talked with you folks?"

"They were here," Rita offered, "but I haven't seen Earl for nearly twenty years and Christopher has never seen him."

"Oh?" Charles responded as his curiosity took over. "How is that?"

Rita Hawkins stood up and said, "If we're going to be talking about Earl, we need to move into the kitchen table and have coffee and a slice of chocolate pie. It's the only way I can stand to talk about the man."

Once they were settled at the kitchen table, Rita began talking about their move from West Virginia back in 1990. "I was pregnant with Christopher and excited about moving closer to my family. I was born here, you know. Well, I guess you don't know that, but this was my home and Earl seemed willing to move here. We bought that little cabin and things seemed fine for a while. Christopher was born that August and, I guess for the first year, I thought everything was okay.

"But it wasn't?" Sarah asked.

"I should have noticed it sooner, but during that year it seemed like Earl became more and more distant. I'd ask him about it and he'd act like it was my imagination. Finally my sister told me she'd seen him in a bar with this woman and they seemed really close. She told me it looked like much more than a fling. I asked him and he didn't bother to deny it. He told me he didn't love me anymore and he wanted to marry this woman.

"Oh Rita," Sarah responded reaching for her hand. "That must have been hard with a new baby..."

"It wasn't as hard as you might think. I was so angry I packed up my stuff and my baby and I went to live with my sister. I refused to see the man, not that he tried all that hard. What really bothered me was that he wasn't interested in the baby at all. He never sent a penny of support."

"How thoughtless," Sarah responded with a deep frown.

"My sister was great about it and the three of us have had a good life. Maude never married and she helped me with Christopher. Once I got a job we did okay. I'm sorry Christopher had to grow up without a father, but he's turned out just fine and he never even asks about his father."

"He seems like a fine young man," Charles interjected. "Very polite and personable."

"You've done a good job," Sarah added.

They chatted about lighter things for the next ten minutes or so until Charles stood and said they should be leaving. They shook hands and as they were leaving, Rita laughed and said, "By the way, I got the last word. I made that man wait nearly twenty years for his divorce. He and his Geraldine couldn't get married and she ultimately ran off with somebody else." She tossed her head back and laughed with pleasure. "I sure got him."

They waved to Christopher as they got into their car. Charles pulled away from the curb but appeared hesitant.

"You seem to be deep in thought. What's going on?" Sarah asked.

"Just thinking, my dear. Just mulling something over." Geraldine. Geraldine. I've seen that name recently...but where?

He slammed on the brake and looked at Sarah with excitement. "Geraldine Nichols," he practically shouted. "Geraldine Nichols and Earl Hawkins -- mother and father of Patrick Henry Nichols. I saw the birth certificate!"

"What has gotten into you?" Sarah asked, looking apprehensive.

"There's another son..." he responded with an exuberant grin.

Chapter 30

"Where did you find him?" Lt. Stokely asked. He and Charles were waiting in his office while the man was being set up in an interview room.

"Nothing to it. I just looked him up in the phone book: Patrick Henry Nichols. He had made no attempt to hide and even when we picked him up, I'd say he seemed relieved.

"That's a strange reaction," Matt responded. "Did he say anything?"

"I told him to wait until he got here so everything was done in an official manner. I didn't want to do anything that might muddy the case."

"Good thinking."

Charles ran through everything that led him to Mr. Nichols, including the dead ends. Lt. Stokely made notes for the record as Charles talked. "I'll need your official report on all this, you know."

"I know, Matt. I know. I'll get that to you tomorrow. What's happening with the guy now?"

"I have Garcia in there questioning him. He's a young guy and I thought he might be able to relate better than us old codgers." He picked up two mugs and filled them from the half-full pot that sat on the side table. Charles imagined that it poured more like syrup than coffee. He took a sip as he left the office and made every effort to control the look on his face.

"Pretty bad, huh?"

They walked up the hall and turned into the room just before the interview room and Matt pulled two chairs up to the back of the one-way mirror. He switched on the speaker.

"So the guy was dead when you got there?"

"That's what I said. He was laying on the floor."

"What did you do?"

"I left."

Garcia sat without speaking and looked at the suspect. Finally he spoke. "Earlier you mentioned a will that left everything to a grandson. How did you happen to see that?"

"I..." he said and then fell quiet.

Finally, Garcia shook his head and stood. "Ok, Patrick. I suggest we start over from the beginning. You've mentioned the will and once you began a sentence with, "He told me..." and now you're saying he was dead when you got there and that you turned around and left and yet somewhere along the way you saw the will. Come on, man. I want to help you, but I can't with you jerking me around like this. You're clearly making this up as you go. I guess I don't understand why you didn't have your story together when we picked you up."

"I knew I hadn't done anything wrong...well, wait, I mean I knew I didn't kill him. I did do something wrong."

"And what was that?"

"I took some money from that guy that wanted to buy the house. It wasn't mine to sell...but it should have been. I guess that was wrong, but I didn't kill the man. He was my father."

"So what did you mean when you started to say, 'He said?'"

Patrick dropped his head. Finally he spoke saying, "That wasn't the first time I was there."

The two men sat quietly for a few minutes until Garcia said, "okay, let's you and me start over from the beginning. Would you like coffee?"

"No thanks."

"Do you mind if I record this time through?"

"I don't mind."

"Do you want a lawyer present?" He had already read the man his rights and he had refused a lawyer.

"No."

Garcia turned on the recorder. "Okay, start from the beginning."

"Which beginning?"

"How about the first time you saw Earl Hawkins."

"I didn't know he was my father. He used to come around when I was a kid but I didn't know until a few months ago when I saw my birth certificate."

"You found your birth certificate?"

"I got it from the county clerk's office. I needed it for the school. I'm going back to school...at least I was before all this," he added dropping his head.

"Okay, so you found out he was your father. Then what?"

"I went to see him. Things were okay at first. We talked. He couldn't explain why he didn't tell me who he was or why he hadn't been around, but he did tell me he was selling the cabin. He told me he was holding out for more money. He said he was going to be a very rich man and that's when I got upset. I told him how mom had struggled over the years, but he didn't seem to care. I tried to get him to agree to give her some of the money when he got it and he told me he was saving it all for his grandson. He said the grandson was the only person that ever cared about him. He even showed me his will and I saw it in black and white. It was all going to the grandson."

"His grandson Travis?"

"Yeah. That's when I learned about this Travis. Ma never told me about him either. I guess I had some family out there..."

Detective Garcia interrupted the young may saying, "so you decided to kill him and pretend to be Travis?"

"No! I told you I did not kill him."

"So what did you do?"

"I didn't do anything for a few months, but then I decided to go back and talk to him again."

"So you went back and got into an argument with him. It was an accident, right? You didn't mean to kill him..." Garcia said attempting to lead the man into a confession.

"I told you he was dead when I got there. I panicked and left. That's all that happened that day."

"But you went back again after that?"

"Yes, after I read in the paper that he'd been found. I went back and obviously no one had moved into the house. I broke in and that's when I came up with the plan. I wasn't sure I could pull it off. I didn't know if people there knew Travis, but I figured it was worth a shot. I was still planning it when those people came by."

"Who was that?"

"I forgot their names. It was a couple and he was a retired cop, I do remember that. That worried me but it turned out to be fine. Actually, we even had a couple of beers together a week or so later. Nice guy."

Matt, on the other side of the mirror looked at Charles, raising his eyebrows. Charles shrugged and said, "You gotta do what you gotta do."

"Anyway," Patrick continued, "once I saw I could get away with pretending to be Travis Hawkins, I contacted that Kirkland fellow. That was harder."

"He didn't believe you were Travis Hawkins?"

"Oh, he believed it all right. He just wanted to go through the process legally, even though he was trying hard to get away with paying the very least for the property. He'd been planning to rip off the old man, so I decided to do the same to him."

"And how were you going to do that? You weren't going to be able to take legal steps to sell the house since you didn't own it."

"I figured that as bad as he wanted it, I could just give him the deed and have him pay me cash. That's what I offered and he bit. I told him it was this or nothing. I walked away with a bundle."

"What did you do with the money?"

"I still have it. I was going to give it to the nursing home as soon as they moved my mother to a private room. Ma's been there three years now. Alzheimer's. She doesn't even know me anymore." He dropped his head again and Garcia respected the moment by remaining silent.

Finally he asked, "Where did you get the deed?"

"Found it right on the old man's dresser. I guess he was thinking about selling when he died."

* * *

"What do you think?" Charles and Sarah were sitting across from one another at their kitchen table. He had just told her the whole story and she sat without speaking when he finished. "Sarah?"

She took a deep breath and finally responded. "Well, I wasn't there, but from what you tell me, Charles, I believe him. How about you?"

"Yeah. I believe the guy. I've spent some time with him and I liked him. At least, I didn't have any bad vibes. He did a stupid thing but for a good reason. He'll go to jail for it if Kirkland presses charges.

"He didn't kill Hawkins, did he?"

"Nah. No chance. The medical examiner was right. Natural causes. Probably brought on by the stress Kirkland was causing and then the son coming out of nowhere. It was all too much for his worn out and abused system."

Sarah sighed again. "I guess I'll call Sophie and let her know it's over."

"Yeah. It's over," he said and added with a note of sadness, "It's completely over."

"What do you mean?"

"I resigned from my contractual work with the department. I decided this would be my last case."

"Oh Charles," she responded, knowing how much he loved his work. "Are you sure?"

"Yep. I could tell with this case. It's time to get on with my life – my retirement life. How about a trip out west?"

"What a great idea!"

Chapter 31

"Sarah," Sophie bellowed as she burst into the house. "Have you been to City Hall?"

"No Sophie, I haven't been there since we went in to get help with the tax bill. What's happened?"

"It's our quilt," she announced excitedly. "It's hanging in the main lobby and someone from the Humane Society is sitting there selling raffle tickets. I bought twenty!"

"Don't you have a bundle of tickets you can sell to yourself?"

"Yes, but I decided to make a big fuss about the quilt and I kept pulling out money and buying more tickets. I attracted quite a crowd," she added proudly.

"I'll bet you did. Did you ask how they're doing?"

"The young girl that was there didn't know, but she said it's going to the library next week."

"Ruth is taking it with her to the Chicago quilt show in a couple of weeks,' Sarah remarked. "She's taking Anna along to sell tickets at her vendor booth. When they get back, it'll be going to the county fair."

"These folks are going to make a killing!" Sophie exclaimed as she pulled off her coat and scarf. "Where's my coffee?"

"Come on into the kitchen. Andy and Caitlyn are already here."

"What's the occasion for this impromptu party anyway?" Sophie asked as she hung her coat in the closet.

"It just seemed like the right time to celebrate all the many changes in our lives – Tim's retirement, Penny and Blossom joining the family, Emma's adoption, the Hawkins' mystery finally laid to rest, Charles' second retirement from the department, and even the completion of the Rescue Quilt."

"I agree," Sophie responded. "This group definitely deserves a party. By the way, who else is coming?"

"Your son, of course, but he called and said he'd be late. I'm not serving dinner until eight so that's fine."

"Dinner at eight? How very cosmopolitan of you!"

Sarah laughed. "Well, this provincial woman here has never been accused of being cosmopolitan. We're only eating late because Charles isn't due back from the airport until late."

"He's picking up his son?"

"Yes, John's plane lands at 6:30 and they should be back here around 7:30."

Andy had just entered the kitchen with a drink in one hand and a plate of cheese and crackers in the other. "John's flying in for the party?" he asked looking surprised.

"Not just for the party. He'll be here tonight," Sarah responded, "but he's coming in to help Patrick and his attorney with their defense."

"I didn't realize he could practice in this state?"

"He can't, but he's a criminal attorney and Charles asked him to come help out. Patrick couldn't afford a lawyer and he's using a court appointed fellow that Charles didn't feel very confident about. He asked his son to come help the guy out."

"Charles really feels for this Patrick guy, doesn't he?"

"Yes, he does," Sarah responded. "The young man is only twenty-five and is watching his mother vanish into the dreadful world of Alzheimer's. She barely knows him anymore. Patrick told Charles that his mother raised him alone with no help from the father. She worked two menial jobs just to get by the whole time he was growing up. Patrick was desperate for the money, but of course that's no excuse for what he did."

"What did he want the money for?"

"Charles said he just wanted to get his mother a private room at the nursing home. She's on assistance and living in a ward with three other indigents."

"That's a sad situation," Sophie responded. She'd been sitting on the couch listening as Sarah talked to Andy. Emma and Barney were laying at her feet. Emma rested her head across Barney's back and both dogs wagged their tails with contented pleasure.

"What about the other son?" Andy asked.

"Christopher will be getting a portion of the inheritance as well once the court gets this whole mess straightened out," Sarah responded.

"What does Charles think will happen to Patrick?"

"John and Charles are going to attempt to get Kirkland to drop the charges. That's really Patrick's only crime and Charles thinks Kirkland won't want the publicity of a trial." The group sat quietly for a few minutes, each lost in their own thoughts.

"Have you told Emma she's been adopted?" Caitlin asked, looking toward Sophie and hoping to lighten the mood.

"I sure have. I told her she's officially one of the family," Sophie responded as she reached down and scratched Emma's ear affectionately. Emma closed her eyes and pushed her head into Sophie's hand.

Suddenly Emma and Barney jumped up and ran to the front door, both barking.

"What's going on?" Andy asked heading toward the door. Just then Tim swung the door wide open and with a swoop of his arm said, "I'd like to present the newest member of our family, Miss Blossom Ward." A tiny black and white pup with large fringed ears came proudly prancing through the door with Penny right behind her.

Once she greeted everyone, Penny scooped the little Papillion into her arms and kissed her on the top of her head. The puppy stretched up and licked Penny's chin but then began wiggling and squirming, eager to get down and play with Emma and Barney who both stood looking baffled.

"With those ears, I can see why she's called the butterfly dog," Andy said.

"Papillion is French for butterfly," Caitlin added, pleased that she could finally use something she had learned in her language class.

Sarah, suddenly realizing Martha was right behind Penny, squealed with delight, "Martha, you're here!"

"I wouldn't have missed it," she responded putting her arm around Penny who was again holding the dog.

Later when Penny and Blossom were sitting with Sarah in the kitchen, Penny spoke up with a little more confidence than usual and said, "I think my Dad likes Martha."

"I think so too," Sarah responded as nonchalantly as she could manage.

"Do you think they'll get married?" Penny asked as she snuggled little Blossom to her chest.

"I don't know," Sarah responded. "What do you think?"

"I don't know either," she said and then added softly, "but I hope so."

Sarah smiled to herself before responding, "Me too."

By the time Charles and John arrived, Blossom was chasing the big dogs around the house, Penny and Caitlin had their heads together sharing a bit of high school gossip, and Sarah sat by the fire sipping wine with her guests and laughing as Sophie entertained them all.

"Life is, indeed, good," Charles said softly to himself.

A Note from the Author

During the writing of this book, Sarah (in the book) and I (in my sewing room) created the quilt described in this book. My quilt was made in memory of my little Shih Tzu, Mollye, and was donated to the Robeson County Humane Society, a no-kill shelter in Lumberton, North Carolina, to be used as a fund raiser.

It is my hope that readers who are members of quilt guilds and clubs, or simply quilters who want to get together with their friends for an old-fashioned sewing bee, will consider making a quilt to benefit their local animal rescue organizations.

Most of these organizations are staffed predominantly by volunteers, and we've all seen their heart-wrenching pleas for donations. They need our help. We may not be able to drive a Pup Mobile like Sophie, or act as mid-wife for pregnant dogs like Bernice, but this is one way each of us can make a difference.

Quilters are always searching for worthwhile charity projects. Who better to help than the creatures who offer us their unconditional love?

Mollye was rescued from a puppy mill in the mid-west where she had been forced to produce litter after litter of little black fluffy pups. After being rescued and placed in a no-kill shelter in Ohio, she was ultimately placed online for adoption.

When I read her story, I knew she belonged with me. I decided I would drive to Ohio from my home in West Virginia to get her, but when I contacted them they apologetically explained that she was no longer there. Due to overcrowding, they had transported her to a foster home in West Virginia.

As it turned out, her new foster home was minutes from my house – *Mollye was on her way to me!*

Mollye and I had seven wonderful years together until her previous lack of care caught up with her. She crossed the *Rainbow Bridge* peacefully at home. I will love her always.

Made in the USA
Lexington, KY
14 January 2016